Marble Hills

Marble Hills

**A Serialized Novel by
Wesley Adams and Daphne McGee**

Book 8 of the Soap Opera Inspired Story Collection
Series Created by Gary Brin

Episodes 1-7

Standish Press

The serialized story in this novel is fiction. Real persons, geographical locations, books, television shows, films, music, and specific events mentioned or which appears as part of the multi-character ensemble in this story were dramatized for entertainment purposes only and have no actual connection to fictional characters and created storylines in this book or reflects upon actual reality of things that may have happened previously or of which seems somewhat similar to real-life situations.

Names of real people mentioned in this book are in bold letters.

Select comments by fictional characters in this novel about historical figures, true crime cases, and, or pop culture icons are based on fact and additional information can be found online in reputable sites as well as numerous published books.

Some characters from the novels *Glass Owl*, *Desperate Lives*, *Thomas Nix*, *Ocean Landing*, *Games People Play* and *Ocean Landing Dangerous Games* appear in this book as part of the continuing storyline. The novels listed are original publications from Standish Press and part of the Soap Opera Inspired Story Collection Series.

In memory of Grace Metalious who wrote *Peyton Place* and inspired many others to write of small town life where nothing is what it appears—and no one is ever happy because of continually focusing on everything but their own shortcomings.

Sometimes the hardest thing to face is reality.

Contents

Intro

Marble Hills is set in and around the small towns in the Camden area of Maine. Like previous novels it exists only in the mind of its readers and not reality. However, like previous novels in this series other locations mentioned are real and do exist. Some of the characters from *Glass Owl* continue their stories within the pages of this novel as they try to adjust to life now that they are more mature and experienced at dealing with life's endless foibles or so it can be assumed anyway. As with other published titles in the Soap Opera Inspired Story Collection Series—characters from existing books will make appearances as part of the continuing storyline to untangle previous plotlines.

Nothing is ever what it seems, and as with previous serialized novels in this series, many of the storylines are taken from real-life events that were reworked into a fictional setting. Nevertheless *Marble Hills* was specifically written to resemble traditional classic soap operas to a certain extent—written with the intention that it was playing to a visual audience and therefore will emulate a scripted format rather than the usual storytelling methods displayed in popular full-length sagas such as *Diamond Head* by Peter Gilman. It should also be noted that each episode of this series were written in a brief span of 6-12 days or less and therefore shouldn't be confused with being great literature. The goal of this serialized series was simply to mimic episodes of prime-time soaps—by creating visual entertainment on a printed page—and not to create a literary masterpiece.

Marble Hills takes place approximately two years after the events in *Ocean Landing Dangerous Games* wrapped. Characters from previous novels in the Soap Opera Inspired Story Collection Series are featured in this book as part of the present story.

Gary Brin
Series Creator

In an effort to have an accurate portrayal of the dialogue used for the *Soap Opera Inspired Story Collection Series* people were anonymously observed in shopping malls, schools, places of employment, and on public streets in order to capture a definitive portrayal of how people of various ages and cultures interacted and talked to each other when they thought no one was listening. While some select dialogue was exaggerated for dramatic purposes when needed—the manner and tone of which people were observed speaking to each other in casual and private conversations is accurate. Exact wording was not copied verbatim for the most part, but the way certain types of topics and conversations are addressed by characters in this serialized series is based on actual situations that were observed over a period of several dozen years.

Prologue

1
Two Months Earlier

A man seems irritated as he looks at a photograph of a woman standing with multiple people in front of a courthouse as reporters stand several feet away with cameras focusing on every word she says. The man grits his teeth and seems enraged.

"She has no right—it should be me."

He clenches his fist.

""Why do you even care?"

The man spins around and faces a woman sitting on a sofa several feet away. He seems ready to pounce on her.

"Did I ask you for your opinion?"

She notices his reaction.

"I don't see why it matters. You don't know her."

He clenches his fist again.

"Shut the fuck up."

He shoots her a warning look.

"Don't push me today—it would be really terrible if that lovely face of yours suddenly needed plastic surgery."

She reacts and stands up suddenly.

"Why does she make you so angry? Is there something you're not telling me about your past—do you know her?"

Without warning the man springs upon the woman and begins choking her. His rage is evident as he throttles her.

2

A woman's body lies motionless on a sofa as a man walks back and forth trying to calm his nerves. He sighs loudly.

"That damn bitch made me kill her."

He gestures with his hand.

"No one will know what happened—I'll wait until dark and dump the body in the ocean. Sharks will take care of her soon enough—by morning there'll be nothing left but scraps."

He begins laughing.

"It wouldn't be the first time I had to think outside the box—took out my college roommate exactly the same way four years ago. It was either that or let that bastard go free—blabbing to everyone what I did to his sister. She had it coming from the start if truth be known. Teasing me with her naked body—telling me she wouldn't give it up to me until she felt like it. Fuck her."

He makes a lewd gesture with his finger.

"But I showed her—forced her to play my game in the shower and afterwards her vicious threats caused me to break her neck and leave her in a wheelchair for life unable to talk."

He looks back at the woman's body on the sofa and wrings his hands nervously. He sighs as he walks over to the sofa.

"She wasn't much of a challenge—broke her neck like a frigging twig. No way for her to tell anyone my secrets."

He begins laughing again.

3

A man quickly drags a garbage bag-covered body through the walkway of a small boat. He slowly looks around and sees no one as shadows of the night dance joyously nearby.

Page **14**

"Uh-huh—sharks are gonna have quite the bloody feast tonight—who knew those brutes could be so helpful?"

He grins broadly and faces the parking lot several yards away. His truck is the only vehicle to be seen. He smirks.

"Hope her family loved her."

The man snickers while he kicks the covered body lying several feet away and snaps his fingers as he glances at the open ocean. He makes a lewd gesture with his hand and laughs.

4

The inky blackness of the fog-covered mists provides a perfect cover as a body splashes onto the waves alongside a boat located several miles from shore. The man looks at his handy work and laughs loudly as the naked body of a woman begins to sink beneath the waves. As he watches the ocean lapping at the battered body he begins laughing again. His joy is evident as he stands there looking at the pitch-black water until the body is completely submerged. He grins as he watches it disappear.

"No one will ever know."

He shakes his hand at the sky.

"Tomorrow I begin phase one of my plan."

He grins slyly and faces the shore again as he slowly walks toward the steering wheel of the boat. He laughs again.

A Brief Look at the First Episode

What seems to everyone like small town perfection is anything but wonderful when a chance meeting between rivals reignite a deadly hatred that threatens to destroy several lives in a small seaside village in southern Maine—as a visitor sparks interest.

Episode 1
Marble Hills

1
Present Day

"Can you believe her nerve?"

Laura McFee shakes her head as she glances at Alice Banning. She seems upset as she faces her husband again.

"It's as if she has no shame."

Matt McFee waves his hand in the air.

"I wish you'd let this go."

Laura shoots him a nasty look.

"I'll just bet you would."

They watch as Alice comes over to where they're sitting.

"Well, well, well—how's tricks."

Laura seems about to explode as she glares at Alice.

"Shouldn't you be slinging hash at that greasy spoon you work at on Market Street? Seriously, who pays your bills?"

Alice makes a lewd gesture with her hand.

"Until a few weeks ago your husband paid all my bills."

She licks her lips sensuously and grins.

"Serviced me really well too—taught me plenty."

She licks her lips again and winks slyly.

"But of course you know that already, don't you."

She laughs and turns to walk out of the coffee shop. Laura clenches her fists as she watches Alice leave. Matt reaches out to touch her hand as she angrily slaps him. He seems upset.

2

As a car drives along a scenic road overlooking jagged cliffs that fall straight down into the ocean, a man smiles broadly as he admires the scenery. He looks at a newspaper lying on the passenger seat with the headline PERFECT SMALL TOWN LIFE IN NEW ENGLAND. As he sees several Victorian houses come into view on the outskirts of a small seaside village he smiles again. The man begins to hum a tune and sighs loudly.

3

"Why can't you just wear a condom when you fuck me?"

Liza Marshall seems upset as she looks at Carter Willington as he begins unbuttoning his Levi's. He rolls his eyes and turns to face her. Liza watches as he climbs into the backseat of his car. He grins as he pulls her toward him. She sighs.

"What if I get pregnant?"

Carter reacts.

"You're not going to get pregnant. Relax already."

He grins broadly.

"I've been with all of your friends. Have they gotten pregnant? You're on the pill. Why should I wear a condom?"

Liza pushes him away.

"You guys are all the same."

Carter laughs.

"Duh—we think with our dicks—deal with it."

He pulls her toward him again.

"Your sister never gives me grief if you must know."

Liza rolls her eyes and seems irritated.

Page 18

"Melissa sleeps around. She slept with your brother if he didn't tell you. Said he was lousy—said he needed lessons."

Carter makes a lewd gesture with his finger.

"My brother has a track record your sister could only hope to have. He's even had a couple of hookers—got it free."

Liza seems disgusted by the comment.

"Ugh—remind me never to sleep with him again."

Carter laughs loudly.

"I'll tell him you said that."

Liza jabs Carter.

"Don't you dare tell Steve I trash-talked him."

Carter grins.

"Oh-oh—is that a bit of fear I hear from you knowing how much influence Steve has over the female population in Marble Hills? My brother can make or break a girl's reputation."

Liza gestures with her hand.

"Not one word."

Carter winks at Liza.

"I'll think about it."

He leans toward her and whispers in her ear. She reacts.

"Ugh—you're a disgusting pig."

He laughs and slides his hand between her legs.

4
Boston

"He did what?"

Jeremy Winterfield looks out the window of his office as he talks on his cell phone. He seems irritated as he sighs.

"Tell him he'd better come around to my way of thinking or there'll be consequences for his stupidity in daring to defy someone like me. I'll expect that fool's answer in one hour."

He grimaces.

"One hour. Then I attack."

He gestures with his hand and laughs.

"You heard me. My reputation speaks for itself."

Page **19**

He clenches his fist and shakes it several times.

"My reputation is what it is because I don't play around with threats. I do as I say. Like I told you earlier, I'll crush his precious company if he refuses to take my demands seriously."

He snaps his fingers as he walks back toward his desk. He smiles broadly and nods several times. He shakes his head.

"Uh-huh—Jeffrey Peller has been served."

He gestures with his hand.

5

Steve Willington grins as he hands a milkshake to Natalie Selleck. He gets into his car and faces her. He smirks slyly.

"You and I have quite a history."

Natalie rolls her eyes.

"Uh-huh—ever since you took my virginity."

Steve laughs loudly.

"You had to lose it to one of us guys anyways."

He gestures with his hand.

"Besides, I was really horny that day and you had no choice but to put out. A guy like me needs a fighter when it comes to sexual exploits. You were a challenge—turned me down plenty of times—spitefully tortured me—but once you realized you couldn't deny me any longer you gave it up willingly."

Natalie shakes her head.

"I remember it differently. Your rep is terrible when it comes to girls in this town—you've been with so many of us—got a few in trouble too—and the sordid incident with that teacher from Blair Street wasn't the best image for a guy like you."

Steve laughs slyly.

"I slept with Linda McFee because I could. Was it my fault that her dope of a husband wasn't handling his duties like he should? I went over to her house and cleaned her pool as she asked—and then one thing led to another and we ended up having uninhibited sex in her bedroom—her husband coming home expectedly was a fluke—he was pissed no doubt."

He leans over to kiss Natalie.

"That jerk tried to kill me. Said I was worthless and that no one would miss me if he took me out. The police said otherwise and locked up the nutjob. I heard he's made plenty of new friends in the slammer. Probably likes dudes now—serves him right."

He begins laughing as Natalie looks at him oddly.

6

"I'm not asking him that—I thought I made it clear."

Jessica Sago glances at the cell phone in her hand and sighs loudly as she sees Marble Hills coming into view.

"Uh-huh—I'm on way as we speak. I'm meeting with him at a coffee shop on Marigold Lane. He'd better be there."

She waves her hand in the air.

"I'll be back in Castle Beach probably around noon."

She nods several times.

7

Castle Beach

Dane Ayler shuts his cell phone off and slowly turns around to face Greg Petrie. He wrings his hands several times.

"We should know more in a few hours."

Greg nods in agreement.

"Jessica Sago is turning out to be quite the reporter."

Dane walks over to where Greg is sitting.

"I agree—hiring her on a trial basis was a smart move way back when—in the time since she's really come into her own."

He wipes sweat from his brow.

"Nevertheless my investment in your newspaper has to get results—I want more edgy stories. I want sales to increase upward from what they've been lately. Updating your website is probably the next item on your agenda you should think about focusing upon—add some video interviews throughout."

Dane looks around the office and shrugs.

Page 21

"Having Eddie Kane as a partner also is really going to infuse this paper with serious potential—turn a tidy profit."

Greg faces the computer and sighs.

8

"Ugh—what if I get pregnant?"

Melissa Marshall slowly pulls away from Patrick Gibbs with an angry look on her face. He begins to laugh as he holds up a broken condom and waves it in the air. He laughs louder.

"I told you I had a big dick."

Melissa makes a lewd gesture with her finger.

"I don't want to have your baby."

Patrick tosses the condom out the car window.

"Who said I wanted you to?"

He wags his finger at her and laughs again.

"But just so you know, there are plenty of girls that would have my baby willingly. I'm quite the catch in case you forgot."

Melissa rolls her eyes.

"Uh-huh—tell that the all the girls you cheated on and then lied about it afterwards. Like I said, I don't want a baby."

Patrick seems annoyed and shrugs.

"What's the big deal anyway? If you get pregnant, get an abortion at that little clinic on Ridgecrest Street. It's not like you've never been with a guy before—especially lately."

She attempts to slap Patrick. He pulls away.

"Ugh—you're no better than your sleazy cousin."

Patrick winks.

"I'll take that as a compliment."

He attempts to pull her toward him again.

"I don't like your attitude lately. You've been acting like you're better than me. Not very attractive if you must know."

Melissa gives him a knowing look.

"Ugh—you sound like a frigging script from that old series *Thirtysomething*—ugh—like get a grip already and face facts about who you are—you're a disgusting toad—troll worthy."

Page **22**

Patrick pulls Melissa toward him and grimaces.

"Who the fuck do you think you are talking to me like I'm some dumbass loser who can't see who you really are—I know what you did with our basketball coach at his beach house."

Melissa seems upset as Patrick grins broadly.

"Uh-huh—I know all about your practice sessions with Coach Holder—seems he knows how to work your engine."

Melissa jerks free of Patrick's grip.

"I don't know what you're talking about."

Patrick begins laughing.

"How about I ask Coach Holder for his take on whether he knows you or not—better yet—why don't I ask his wife?"

Melissa angrily glares at Patrick.

9

The isolated beach at the end of a lonely road is quiet except for two teenagers fighting by the surf. They seem to be in a heated argument as the teenage girl angrily slaps the teenage boy and begins walking toward a car parked not far away. He follows and forcibly grabs her. They begin fighting once more.

10
Boston

"I'm on my way—it isn't the end of the world."

Jeremy seems upset and sighs loudly as he walks toward a car in an underground parking lot. He shakes his head as he pulls out a set of keys from his pants pocket. He stops and turns.

"Enough already—tell her I'm on my way."

He shuts off his cell phone and seems upset.

"Ex-wives like Evelyn can seriously test a guy's willpower when it comes to doing the right thing. If it wasn't for Andrea there'd be no reason to ever talk to that woman again."

He turns to face Andrew Latimer.

"Do yourself a favor—never marry."

Andrew grins broadly.

"Not every woman is like your ex—I marvel at the fact you dealt with her that long before you finally called it quits."

Jeremy knowingly rolls his eyes.

"She wasn't all bad at first—but she slowly became someone I didn't know and couldn't live with. Luckily Andrea is enrolled at Pinecrest and gets some time away from her mother's extreme behavior. Too bad for her new boyfriend—he's not so lucky when it comes to her erratic moods. I almost feel sorry for Jackson—but not entirely. He's a sucker for punishment."

Andrew looks at Jeremy curiously.

"Did Jackson say why Evelyn needed to speak to you?"

Jeremy shakes his head.

"Not really."

He rolls his eyes again.

"Jackson is probably ready for the funny farm if truth be known. Two months already and he's a frigging basket case."

He laughs.

"Better him than me I guess."

Andrew nods in agreement and sighs.

"When should I expect you back?"

Jeremy shrugs.

"I'm done for the day."

Andrew nods.

11

"I'll see you tomorrow."

Liza nods as she turns around to look at Carter. He grins slyly and makes a lewd gesture with his finger. He laughs.

"My brother will probably call you later."

Liza seems uneasy.

"Don't you dare tell him what I said earlier?"

Carter grins.

"You and I have to work out an arrangement that is seriously beneficial to my penis—it would only be fair."

Liza rolls her eyes.

"You're a pig."

"Uh-huh—that crack is gonna cost you plenty."

Carter makes a lewd gesture with his finger and winks.

"It would be such a shame if Steve knew what I heard earlier. He would be seriously displeased with your attitude."

Liza reacts as Carter starts the engine of his car.

"I thought we had a deal?"

"Some deals are meant to be broken."

She watches as he drives away.

12

"We're over. Get used to it."

Ashley Brewster glares at Robert Campo briefly before running toward her car a few feet away. She stops suddenly.

"I'm not that type of girl."

She sighs loudly.

"I'm done with you. Stop calling me or I'll tell my brother what you did to me—he's coming from college in a few days."

Ashley smiles slyly.

"My brother hates you by the way."

Robert seems bored by Ashley's comment.

"Fuck you and your brother. I'm *so* over you."

He watches her as she fumbles with the keys to her car. He runs his fingers through his hair and sighs loudly.

13

"Uh-huh—an equal partner seems about right, Dane. Of course I can help you out if you agree to my terms. I already own one newspaper as you know—so what's one more? Yeah—but that's not how I do business as you already know—I'm hands on all the way—got to protect my investment if I see potential in your newspaper. Expect my input from the getgo—tell Petrie what I expect from him too—no use to pretend at this point."

Eddie Kane rolls his eyes and seems pleased.

"Tomorrow works perfectly for me."

He gestures with his hand.

"No problem. I'll be in my office."

Eddie grins as he gestures with his hand once more.

"I'll expect you at nine."

He sighs loudly as he shuts off his cell phone and leans back in his chair. He smiles broadly and faces his computer.

14

Several teenagers are standing by a car parked not far away from the entrance of a deserted beach house.

"I still think we should throw a party here on Saturday."

Kelvin Penney points to the house and sighs.

"No one will care. Place is empty."

He looks at the entrance and smiles broadly as Bruce Holland shoots him a cautious look. Kelvin turns away.

"It's either here or we forget about it altogether."

He reaches out to shove Bruce.

"Of course when everyone finds out you guys wimped out there won't be a way to save your reps. Imagine the talk."

Lyle Lincoln and Timothy Bradley look at each other.

"Who said anything about wimping out?"

Kelvin glances at the house again and grins broadly.

"It is what it looks like."

Lyle walks over to where Kelvin is standing.

"Who's gonna pay for it?"

Kelvin grins.

"I am."

Timothy seems confused.

"Is that so?"

Bruce begins laughing.

"Do tell. I heard you got cleaned out by some lawyer that your father made an enemy of before he kicked the bucket."

Kelvin clenches his fist as he glares at Bruce.

"Who said I don't have any money—got plenty. More than you think if you must know—I'm loaded with plenty cash."

Bruce gestures with his hand wildly.

"Says who?"

He begins laughing loudly.

"That lawyer cleaned out your family and left you and your sister without any money—uh-huh—pretty rough deal."

Kelvin seems enraged and faces Bruce.

"My father left me plenty."

Bruce glances at Lyle and Timothy with a knowing look before he faces Kelvin once again. Kelvin sighs loudly.

"That frigging asshole talked trash about my family. I'm not poor. My lawyer is gonna sue Jeremy Winterfield."

Bruce gives Kelvin a knowing look.

"Explain the fact you live with your housekeeper."

Kelvin seems upset.

"She's not my housekeeper. She's my aunt."

Lyle points at Kelvin.

"Uh-huh—yeah—I'll just bet she's your aunt. Except of course everyone in Marble Hills knows your deal—knows what happened in Castle Beach a few years back. It was quite the story no doubt. Cable news had a field day. CNN was running stories for weeks on what happened to your brother and father."

Kelvin angrily clenches his fist once more.

"My father suffered a crippling stroke after Chandler passed away suddenly. It could happen to anyone. It happened to an old movie star named **Debbie Reynolds** when her daughter **Carrie Fisher** died suddenly. Losing her daughter caused her to have a massive stroke and she died less than a day later."

Lyle seems bored.

"Wasn't that chick the one from *Star Wars*?"

Kelvin nods.

"Uh-huh—*anyway* after my father died, my sister and I decided to live with Melora Schubb. We moved to Marble Hills to be closer to her sister—not because of any other reason."

Bruce winks at Lyle and Timothy.

"Likely story no doubt. Unfortunately I have it on good authority that your explanation is a figment of your extremely wild imagination. You're hurting for money—no longer sporting a trust fund like before—Winterfield royally stripped you bare."

He begins laughing loudly.

"I heard what Jeremy Winterfield did to your estate after your father croaked. That guy is one nasty motherfucker. I heard he carved up your father's money and gave most of it to some old dude named Orville Pendergraft—enjoyed doing it too."

Kelvin shrugs.

"You're a fucking asshole, Bruce. No wonder you can't get laid. Who would be dumb enough to spread for you?"

Bruce glances at Lyle and Timothy.

"Ask your sister—she knows plenty about my skills in the backseat of your housekeeper's car—plowed her plenty."

Kelvin suddenly takes a swing at Bruce.

15

"I'm not gonna wait forever for you to spread your legs."

Eden Penney turns to face Denver Skiffington with an angry glare. She watches as he tugs at the belt buckle of his faded Levi's and grins. He begins to unbutton his jeans and smirks.

"There are endless girls I could be with at this very minute. I didn't get the rep I have for patiently waiting to get laid."

Eden walks over to where Denver is standing by several large boulders leading to a stretch of sandy beach about ten yards to the east. She stops and glances at her car and then back at Denver. She seems irritated as he grins broadly at her.

"What's the big deal anyway—it's not like we haven't fucked before—you've given it up plenty in the past year."

Eden reacts to the comment.

"You promised me you wouldn't have sex with Mariska Benson—said you'd respect my wishes about her. Said you heard she was sloppy in the sack—then you slept with her anyway."

Denver makes a lewd gesture with his finger.

"I lied—like deal already."

He pulls Eden toward him and grins.

"You girls are just too damn competitive if truth be known—always trying to best each other with us guys."

He glances down at his erect penis.

"Mariska has the same attitude about you—said you're a tramp—said you've slept around with every guy in town."

Eden reaches out to stroke Denver's exposed penis.

"She projects her behavior onto me. It's she who has slept with every guy in Marble Hills. Ask anyone—she's trash."

Denver waves his hand in the air.

"Enough already—I'm not impressed with your obvious ploys to get my attention where Mariska is concerned."

He glances at his penis again.

16

Elizabeth Pendleton shuts the door to her car and turns to face the street across from Springview Mall. She smiles as she sees David Sawyer coming toward her from his car. He waves.

"Traffic in Marble Hills is terrible."

Elizabeth shrugs.

"Tell me something I don't know."

They face the mall.

"Eddie wants to know what we think about renovating Springview. He's not happy with how it's being managed."

David shakes his head.

"Well, I guess we might as well pay a visit to Simone Holland. She won't be pleased to see us—count on it."

Elizabeth shrugs.

"Do you think Eddie is going to fire her?"

David shakes his head.

"I don't know. Ever since I began working for my brother I've come to see many facets of his personality. He can be quite nice but he can also be ruthless. He doesn't play games."

Elizabeth nods in agreement and shrugs.

Page **29**

"I've known him all my life and I've never caught him lying about anything. What you see is what you get with Eddie."

David stops and faces Elizabeth.

"I guess we're really lucky he hired us right out of college. He could've gone with more experienced candidates?"

Elizabeth wipes sweat from her brow.

"We have Gina Bentley to thank. She put in a good word for us a month ago—and surprise—we both have jobs."

David glances at his watch.

"I can still recall the first time I met her. She was seriously freaked about the fact I was Brad McKinley's long-lost twin."

Elizabeth laughs.

"I remember that day like it was yesterday. She stared at you for a whole minute—speechless—couldn't say a word."

She reaches out to touch David's hand.

"Finding out Brad had a twin was a shock to Gina but finding out the two of you were half-siblings was even more of a shock. Gina had been through a lot at that point and somehow she held it all together despite realizing the truth about her identity and yours too for that matter. Eddie on the other hand took it in stride. He accepted reality without question."

David gestures with his hand.

"Finding out he was my half-brother was something no doubt—told me outright he hated our biological father and would never accept the fact they were related despite knowing the truth decades after—but said he didn't hold anything against Blake Madison's victims. Made it clear my mother was one of Madison's many victims. It was quite the eye-opener for yours truly."

Elizabeth gives David a curious look.

"How *is* your mother?"

David shrugs.

"I guess she's alright. She still seems confused about what was done to her at the hospital. Other than that she's accepted the fact that I wasn't stillborn—and that Brad is dead."

Elizabeth reaches out to touch David's hand again.

17

"I swear I'm gonna kill that skanky bitch."

Laura slams the door shut behind her as she turns to face Matt. He watches her for a few seconds and sighs loudly.

"It's over—there's nothing to worry about."

Laura grabs Matt by the arm.

"That whore isn't going to give up chasing you. She wants you back in her bed. She made that quite clear with her actions earlier. She's determined to destroy my marriage so she can have you for herself. But I've got plans for her—deadly plans."

Matt rolls his eyes.

"What exactly are you going to do, Laura? Drown her at Bradford Beach? Cut the brakes to her car? Shoot her?"

Laura grins slyly.

"I've got something much worse in mind."

Matt seems upset.

18

"I'm going to buy another pack of condoms for our date tomorrow—a guy has to be prepared—if he wants to get laid."

Patrick grins and watches Melissa's reaction as she slams the door shut to his car. He blows her a kiss and smirks.

"See you tomorrow at eight."

Melissa watches as Patrick drives away. She sighs loudly.

"Ugh—can he get any worse?"

She hears someone clapping and turns around.

"I see you've been sampling my leftovers yet again."

Marlene Benson makes a lewd gesture with her hand and grins broadly as she sees Melissa's reaction. She takes a step forward as Melissa rolls her eyes. They glare at each other.

"Didn't I see you earlier today with your tongue down some old dude's throat—seems he couldn't catch his breath."

Marlene appears about to explode and sighs.

"Zane Withers is only thirty-seven."

Page **31**

She takes another step and suddenly stops.

"You're just mad because I got myself a real man and you're still playing around with boys—oh, how sad for you."

Melissa licks her lips seductively.

"Wonder what will happen when his wife finds out her husband has been playing around with a college student?"

Marlene waves her hand in Melissa's face.

"If she finds out I'll be forced to tell your mother that your slug of a father fucked that slut from that filthy diner on Market Street two days ago during his lunch break—what's her name again? Oh, that's right, I almost forgot—Alice Banning—bet you anything she has an STD. Imagine what would happen if I were to spill what I know? This would end really badly—deadly."

Melissa shakes her head.

"I don't know what you're talking about."

Marlene laughs knowingly.

"Uh-huh—we'll see about that."

She waves her hand in Melissa's face again and circles her with a wicked grin. Marlene licks her lips knowingly.

"One word from me and your father could find himself in the morgue with a bullet in his head courtesy of your freak of a mother. Didn't she get taken away to the nuthouse last year?"

Marlene smiles broadly as she walks away.

19

Simone Holland slowly leans back in her chair as she glances at Elizabeth and David nervously. She sighs loudly.

"Springview has been a challenge as you know. Ever since Kane Enterprises took over I've tried to get things up to standard in order to be competitive. But store owners aren't willing to change how they do business. I don't know what else to do."

David gestures with his hand.

"I think you do."

Simone seems confused.

20

"I didn't know you were coming over today?"

Eddie hugs Gina Bentley warmly and turns to look at the window overlooking a massive lawn below. He smiles.

"I thought I'd pop in and see how you were doing."

Gina rolls her eyes.

"I'm fine—got the best big brother in the world to show me the way—keep me from making a total fool of myself."

Eddie waves his hand in the air. He glances at the door for a few seconds. He notices her reaction and smiles broadly.

"You're doing just fine."

He closes the door behind him and sighs.

"I thought you'd like to see this."

He pulls out a rolled newspaper from his jacket.

"Seems John Bentley had a biological child after all—her name is Erin McHenry. She lives in Boston. She intends to sue for what's left of Bentley's estate—got herself a lawyer already."

Gina looks at the headline on the front page.

"Who's her lawyer?"

Eddie wipes sweat from his brow.

"Warren Manning."

Gina reacts.

21

"Your attitude has certainly improved since you moved back to Marble Hills from New Haven. Nice move."

Susan Ingalls winks at Trey Holder.

"Uh-huh—you've also taught me how much a man's penis can give incredible pleasure to a women when he knows what he's doing—even when he's stuck in a miserable marriage."

Trey laughs as he kisses Susan.

"Carissa just doesn't understand my moods—never has actually. My marriage is in name only for all intense purposes."

Susan slides her fingers across his lips and grins.

Page **33**

"Your wife is a fool—her loss is my gain—hiring you to coach my daughter's basketball team was a stroke of genius on my part. You're not only a good basketball coach but you've taught me plenty in the bedroom as well—if only my husband had been as good as you—before left town with our babysitter."

She seems annoyed and shrugs.

"I should've known he was fooling around by how happy he began acting when that damn slut showed up wearing a white see-through blouse that said tramp all over it. Two weeks later I caught them together in our bed—fucking like rabbits."

Trey laughs loudly.

"Man had balls regardless—to fool around right under your nose—no doubt he wanted to be rid of his marriage."

Susan kisses Trey again.

"That nasty tramp and my ex live in Bangor now—moved in with her parents. Ugh—can you imagine anything worse?"

Trey grins and pulls Susan toward him.

"I assume you know I haven't been faithful to you, right? I've played. Carissa could never control me—cheated on her before we were married and after—but she doesn't suspect that I've strayed again. She thinks I'm faithful like a church mouse."

Susan laughs and strokes his cheek.

"I don't own you—you're a married man—you have to do what serves your purpose when the moment strikes you."

She slides her fingers across his lips again.

"Besides I've heard of your exploits all over town. You have a rep—bad boy galore. Your wife must have blinders."

Trey begins laughing and points at Susan.

22

Melora Schubb glances at her watch again as she faces her sister. She turns to look at the window fronting the sidewalk.

"This is certainly not good news."

Megan Vanderpoole shakes her head.

"I think it's time you face reality before it's too late."

Page **34**

They look at each other for a few seconds.
"Did the doctor say how much time you have left?"
Megan shrugs.
"She doesn't know."
Melora wipes sweat from her brow.
"There's nothing she can do?"
Megan shakes her head.
"It's inoperable."
Melora reaches out to hug her sister.
"I love you."
They look at each other again.
"Have you told Alvin?"
Megan shakes her head and seems worried.

23

"Simone took it better than expected."
Elizabeth turns to face David.
"Uh-huh—but she's so doomed regardless."
David shakes his head and sighs.
"Or she's really clueless when it comes to bad news?"
Elizabeth turns to look back at Springview Mall as they walk down the sidewalk. She shakes her head several times.
"She'll probably find another job easily."
David gives Elizabeth an odd look.
"We'll see."
He stops and looks at her.
"I've been thinking of sending my mother on a cruise."
Elizabeth seems confused.
"Your mother isn't the cruise type."
David pulls out his cell phone and begins dialing.
"What about a bed and breakfast deal up the coast?"
Elizabeth nods.
"She might like that."
He stops dialing.
"I just want to do something nice for her."

Page **35**

He wrings his hands nervously.

"She has been through a bit of a rough patch in the last few years. First she finds out about me and then the truth about what happened to my twin brother got revealed in the worst way when Archie Spaulding snapped and had to be admitted to one of those hospitals in Portland that deal with mentally ill people."

Elizabeth shoots David a knowing look.

"Brad McKinley got what he deserved from Archie Spaulding. Granted it was a horrible way to die but Brad brought that upon himself for killing Carrie Spaulding. Sealing him inside that creepy room was justice served as far as I'm concerned. Then Carrie's dad began blabbing to anyone who would listen that he had seen Carrie at his house—saying that she spoke to him—had to be led away in a straightjacket after he tried to kill you on Peabody Avenue—kept screaming about you being dead."

David sighs loudly.

"That was a really scary moment for me. He must have thought I was Brad—kept saying I had to die for what I did."

Elizabeth shakes her head several times.

24

"Damn bitch—I think it's time she figured out who's calling the shots. Bursting her bubble will be quite the moment."

Melissa clenches her fist.

"Marlene Benson had better watch her back."

She laughs slyly.

"There's nothing worse than a woman with plenty of secrets just waiting to be exposed at the worst possible moment by someone who won't feel the least bit sorry—oh yeah."

She looks at her cell phone.

"I think it's time everyone in town know she gave Father Vincent a blowjob. The look on his face that day said plenty."

She begins dialing.

"Oh my—what will people say?"

Melissa licks her lips and begins laughing.

Page 36

"Who pissed on your party?"

Patrick turns around and faces Timothy as he sits down at the corner booth inside a small diner. They look at each other.

"Oh wait—don't tell me—you crossed paths with that wretched bitch again—and she played you once more."

Patrick rolls his eyes.

"That whore is gonna be the death of me."

Timothy makes a lewd gesture with his finger.

"Why do you even bother with Melissa Marshall? She's got a foul attitude. Always scheming—causes trouble every chance she gets—no one is safe whenever she's around—dark cloud."

Patrick gives Timothy a knowing look.

"Uh-huh—you don't like her because she refused to spread her legs for you when you asked—called you a dork."

Timothy recoils.

"Like I care what that slut thinks?"

He laughs.

"I can do better."

Patrick gestures with his hand.

"So says you."

He leans back in the booth.

"She and I had words earlier—made it look like I was just out for a good time—didn't care about her feelings."

Timothy jabs Patrick.

"Seems to me she got it right about you—hit that one right on the mark—uh-huh—bet that stung a bit afterwards."

"Who asked you?"

Patrick turns to at the counter where the owner Lacey Arlington is talking to someone he doesn't recognize.

"Seems Lacey got herself a new squeeze?"

Timothy glances at the counter.

"Doubt it—she's still hung up on her dead hubby."

Patrick grins broadly and gestures.

"Dude died last year in an accident—fell off that new building on Seaview Avenue. It's time for her to find someone else to keep her warm at night before she loses her looks."

Timothy reacts and stands up.

"I'll see you later."

Patrick looks at Timothy oddly.

"Say hi to your charming sister for me."

"Uh-huh—I will."

He heads toward the door as Patrick glances at Lacey and grins as he sees her smiling broadly. He shakes his head.

"Get a room already."

He picks up a menu and shrugs.

26

Trey kisses Susan one more time as he shuts the door to his car. He grins as he looks at her and wags his finger slyly.

"Nice way to spend an afternoon."

Susan smirks.

"I'd say—you came twice."

Trey makes a lewd gesture with his finger.

"I'll call you tomorrow."

Susan nods.

"I'll be waiting."

She watches as he winks and drives away.

"He's something special no doubt."

She turns around and notices Melissa looking at her from across the street. She mouths the words "I know" to Susan.

27

Lacey looks at the newspaper and at several photographs displayed on the counter top—and sighs. She faces Alan McGyver with a puzzled look on her face. He seems upset and shrugs.

"I thought everyone knew about Point Blye?"

Lacey shakes her head.

Page 38

"I'm new to this area. Lived most of my life just down the way in Paradise Point—moved here just over a year ago."

Alan looks at the photographs again.

"Any suggestions on someone who might know about the house—it has history—plenty of drama I'm assuming?"

They look at each other.

"You might try the local library."

Alan runs his fingers through his hair.

"I've been there already—no one knows anything."

Lacey reaches out to pat Alan's hand lightly.

28

David seems pleased as Marvella DuBois wraps her arms around his waist and kisses him several times. He grins.

"I gather you missed me?"

Marvella jabs David in the chest.

"What do you think?"

She hugs him again.

"How's Elizabeth?"

David shakes his head.

"She's fine."

Marvella seems upset and sighs.

"Eddie called—wanted to know how things went with Simone Holland at the Springview Mall earlier—curious."

David gestures with his hand.

"Took care of it already—he's satisfied with the fact she's open to accepting help from yours truly. Simone Holland is not what I expected. She's sort of reserved—very bookish."

Marvella runs her fingers through David's hair and shoots him a look. He notices and begins laughing. He shrugs.

"She's dedicated—maybe too much."

Marvella seems confused.

"What's that supposed to mean?"

David walks toward the kitchen and stops. He seems to think for a moment and then faces Marvella once more.

"Exactly what it sounded like—she probably hasn't had a date in years—worried too much about Springview Mall."
Marvella walks over to David.
"Did Elizabeth see what you saw?"
David shrugs.
"Don't know—why don't you ask her yourself?"
Marvella jabs David playfully.

Two Days Later

29

"Are you going jogging right now?"
Matt turns to look at Laura. She scowls at him.
"Uh-huh—why?"
She walks over to where he is standing. She eyes his clothing and seems upset. He notices and rolls his eyes.
"What's wrong?"
Laura seems irritated.
"Do you have to wear shorts that tight?"
Matt notices her anger.
"What's wrong with what I'm wearing?"
Laura wags her finger at Matt.
"If you cheat on me again—we're through."
Matt rolls his eyes.
"Why can't you forget what happened with Alice? It's old news. Tired and boring. It's over and done with. Let it be."
Laura grabs Matt's arm.
"When you get back we have to talk."
Matt reacts.
"I'll be back in an hour."
Laura looks at Matt's clothing once more as her eyes fall on the massive bulge in his snug-fitting shorts. She sighs.
"Don't be late."
Matt seems upset and leaves. Laura watches the door close and runs to the window. She stops and turns around.

Page **40**

"Why can't he wear regular shorts to go jogging? Seems to me there's only one reason he's wearing shorts that tight."

She clenches her fist.

"If he starts up with that damn whore again I'll kill her. I swear I'll put a bullet in that miserable slut's head if she dares to start sniffing around my husband again—enough is enough."

She looks at a photo of her and Matt together.

30

"What's wrong Melora?"

Eden watches as Melora turns away and seems upset for some reason. Eden reaches out to grab Melora's arm.

"What's going on?"

Melora turns around and sighs loudly.

"It's my sister."

Eden seems confused.

"Is your sister all right?"

Melora turns away again and seems about to cry. Eden notices and reaches out again. They look at each other.

TO BE CONTINUED

A Brief Look at the Second Episode

A woman tries to find more about her secret past while several relationships continue to deteriorate even further—creating chaos in the present as an unfaithful husband strays once more.

Episode 2
Change of Heart

1
Boston

"I want to meet my half-sister."

Erin McHenry faces Warren Manning with a determined look on her face. She walks over to where he is sitting. He seems confused and looks at the paperwork on his desk. He sighs.

"Gina Bentley isn't your half-sister."

Erin waves her hand in the air and shrugs.

"I don't do details."

Warren gives her a knowing look.

"At best Gina is your stepsister. One that she never knew she had until just a few short days ago. Let it sink in a bit."

Erin points her finger at Warren.

"I won't be ignored."

Warren stands up and glances at the door.

"How about we talk about this further over lunch? We have a lot to discuss where your lawsuit is concerned."

Erin nods and watches as Warren comes toward her.

"What kind of person is she?"

Warren shrugs and seems uneasy.
"She's been through a lot."
Erin points her finger at Warren again.
"So have I."
Warren nods in agreement.

2

"Is your sister gonna die?"
Melora Schubb seems shocked as Eden Penney reaches out to touch her hand. Melora pulls away and sighs loudly.
"Her doctor doesn't seem to think she has a chance other than to face reality that she doesn't have much time left."
Eden seems upset at the comment.
"Can't they try some new drug or something?"
Melora shakes her head.
"She's tried everything available."
Eden reaches out and hugs Melora warmly.
"Is there anything I can do?"
Melora shakes her head and grimaces.

3

Marla Sherwood angrily rolls her eyes as she looks at her boyfriend standing a few feet away from her. She shrugs.
"I thought I told you I'm not ready."
Christian Keller seems irritated and sighs.
"I don't understand why you're acting this way."
Marla gives Christian a knowing look.
"I said I'm not ready and I meant it."
Christian runs his fingers through his hair.
"I'm the only frigging virgin in my class. We've been dating for six months already. Let's just fuck and be done with it."
Marla opens to the door to Christian's car.
"I'm *so* out of here."
She angrily slams the door shut and faces him.

Page **44**

"I'm not like the other girls in this town. I have morals and I'm not putting out because you want to lose your virginity."

She watches his reaction and sighs.

"You'll just have to deal with it."

Christian gestures with his hand and sighs.

"Do you think you're better than me because you lived in Boston for a while? Or is it Pinecrest Prep? That school is not all that in case you thought it was. You're no better than me."

Marla wags her finger at Christian.

"None of what you said has anything to do with my choice in losing my virginity. For the record I'm from Marble Hills—got plenty of roots here as well as Castle Beach down the coast. I just need more time before I decide exactly what's right for me."

She glances at the street up ahead.

"If you can't wait, too bad, go find some other girl to stick your virgin dick into. There's plenty here in Marble Hills."

Christian starts the engine of his car.

"Maybe I will."

He sighs loudly and drives away. Marla watches him slowly drive away and turns to face the sidewalk once more.

"Who does he think he is anyway?"

She pulls out a compact mirror from a pocket in her oversized jacket. She looks at herself briefly and shrugs.

4
Boston

Jeremy Winterfield leans back in his chair as he talks on his cell phone. He seems upset as he listens. He sits up.

"I thought we had that cleared up Jackson. I'm not going to deal with your dirty laundry concerning my ex. You knew the deal when you started to date her. You were duly warned."

He nods several times.

"I think it's time you bailed."

He stands up and walks over to the window.

"Uh-huh—you heard right—I said it."

Page 45

He turns around and stops suddenly. He shrugs.

"Cut your losses before it's too late."

He nods a few times and shuts off the cell phone. From outside his office he hears loud shouting. He walks to the door and opens it to see Andrew Latimer arguing with a man dressed in an expensive suit. They turn to look at him. He sighs.

"This is for you."

The man throws a sealed envelope toward Jeremy and smirks slyly. He faces Andrew briefly and then Jeremy again. Jon Melchoir grins broadly as he watches Jeremy's reaction.

"What the fuck is this?"

Jon grins broadly.

"You've been put on notice."

He turns to leave without another word.

5

"You're not going get away with this Marvin. I won't let you get one over on me. No way will it happen. I swear."

Marvin Houston grins broadly and quickly pulls Elizabeth Pendleton toward him. He kisses her. They begin laughing.

"You've got no game when it comes to me. I'm much too charming—got things all figured out. It's what it is—deal."

Elizabeth slides her fingers along Marvin's cheeks.

"You've made me so happy in the last year. I never thought I'd ever find someone like you—someone so nice."

Marvin grins broadly.

"You just had that spark I like."

Elizabeth pulls Marvin toward her and kisses him.

"Have you ever been with a black girl?"

Marvin shakes his head.

"No—I've just always liked white women. Nothing wrong with black women though. I'm just attracted to white women."

They look at each other.

"It was a shock for your parents when they met me. I could see they expected someone different—someone white."

Elizabeth waves her hand in the air.

"They were shocked, but after meeting you they changed their tune. My mother especially liked you. Said you were really handsome—said you'd make pretty babies. Liked how polite you were—treated me with respect—showed them respect too."

Marvin laughs and kisses Elizabeth again.

"I was raised in a house of women. My father bailed when I was three. Never saw him again. My mother and grandmother raised me and my sister alone. Taught me to respect my elders before everything else—made me appreciate being loved."

Elizabeth strokes Marvin's cheek again.

"Would you ever want to see your father again?"

Marvin shakes his head.

"Doesn't matter to me now—I have no memory of what he looked like—can't remember him at all if truth be known."

"You don't have a photo of him?"

Marvin shakes his head again.

"He left nothing behind but a bunch of unpaid bills."

Elizabeth seems upset as she wraps her arms around Marvin. They look at each other again. She kisses him.

"I'm really glad we met that day."

She seems about to cry.

"Who'd ever think a guy in faded ripped jeans and a T-shirt that said SEX IS SIMPLY EXERCISE WITHOUT LOVE could turn out to be such a wonderful boyfriend to someone like me?"

Marvin looks at Elizabeth curiously.

"What happened when you were in high school is old news. I don't judge. I only know the person you are now."

Elizabeth wipes a tear from her eye and sighs.

"You're just too perfect for words."

Marvin grins and makes a lewd gesture with his finger.

"Perfect my ass—I've had my share of issues too."

He pulls out a batch of parking tickets from the back pocket of his jeans. He waves them around for a few seconds.

"I've got one for each month of the year."

He points to a few of them.

"Your boyfriend is no saint by any means."

"Aren't you going to pay them?"

Marvin waves the tickets around again before shoving them into the back pocket of his jeans. He grins slyly.

"I paid them this morning before visiting my mother in Boston—she'd kill me if I didn't play nice with the law."

Elizabeth seems confused and shrugs.

6

"Uh-huh—you and me aren't over by any means."

Steve Pendleton grins broadly as he pulls a woman toward him and kisses her. Yvette Vanderpoole pretends to be annoyed as he laughs loudly. He lies back in bed and seems pleased.

"What would your wife say?"

Steve laughs again.

"She'd slice my dick off without a second thought with the biggest knife she could find. She takes her vows seriously."

Yvette wags her finger at Steve.

"If my parents knew I was fooling around with a man half my age they'd disown me. They'd die if they knew the truth."

Steve makes a lewd gesture with his finger.

"It was your fault that I strayed—you pranced around the pool in practically nothing at my daughter's summer party last year—teased me. Made it clear you wanted something extra."

Yvette rolls her eyes and climbs out of bed.

"I'm twenty. I can sleep with who I want. You're a hot guy for someone your age. Late thirties is just the right age as far as I'm concerned. Besides you didn't exactly tell me to back off."

Steve climbs out of bed and walks over to Yvette.

"You get me in ways my wife can't. She hardly looks at me anymore. I'm a virile guy—I want to fuck—want to fuck a lot."

Yvette gives Steve a knowing look.

"I wasn't the first woman to cause you to break your marriage vows—you've been around quite a bit. Women talk plenty—they say you have tons of game—lots of stamina."

Page 48

Steve pulls Yvette toward his naked body.

"OK—OK—I'm strayed plenty. I stopped being faithful on my honeymoon. Slept with the captain's daughter—she dared me to drop my shorts at the gym and I did—then we fucked."

Yvette leans forward and kisses Steve.

"What's my deal? Are gonna dump me when something better comes along. Coldly ignore me whenever we meet?"

Steve winks slyly at Yvette.

"I've been there and done that plenty—and yeah, I like you but so what—I'm taken. What do you want from me? I'm a married man after all—till death do us part and all that crap."

Yvette pushes Steve away.

"I don't like your wife. Dump her."

Steve gestures with his hand.

"I can't do that."

"Why can't you get rid of that miserable shrew?"

Steve seems upset and turns away.

"I just can't. I won't."

Yvette licks her lips.

"I want more than a fling from you. I think I'm in love with you, Steve Pendleton. I want to have children with you."

They look at each other for a few seconds.

"A boy and a girl would be nice—twins perhaps."

Steve runs his fingers through his hair.

"I have kids already—or did it slip your mind?"

Yvette licks her lips again.

"I want you to father my children."

She looks at his naked body.

"I won't take no for an answer no matter your excuses."

Steve glances back at the bed and sighs.

"I'm not father material. I've done a lousy job with the kids I have. Ask anyone. My kids think I'm a failure. Ask them."

Yvette waves her hand in the air.

"I know all about how your daughter feels about you and don't get me started on your stupid son. Ugh—he used me."

Steve grabs his shirt from a chair nearby.

"Uh-huh—don't for a second think I don't know you slept with my son plenty before we hooked up—he has a rep too."

Yvette glances at the door. She seems upset.

7
Boston

Jeremy paces around his office in a rage as Pierce Colby stares at him blankly. He waves a file in the air and sighs.

"I'm not going to stand for that snot-nosed lawyer talking to me like I'm a zero—he's going to regret tangling with me."

Pierce shakes his head.

"Even from the grave Carson Penney is being a royal pain in the ass—I guess it's back to the courtroom for you."

Jeremy stops and faces Pierce.

"I had every right to drain the Penney children of every last dollar they had—Orville Pendergraft wasn't the only victim of Carson's wretched spawn. Chandler Penney raped and killed Ivy Patterson right before he met his end—and her family deserved a settlement that wasn't going to insult their daughter's memory after what happened. Was it my fault Penney was a terrible businessman that left a whole slew of unpaid bills? When the IRS got through with the Penney estate there was hardly anything left for the younger Penney children to inherit. Heard everything turned out decent for them regardless—they went to live with their former maid in Marble Hills right after Penney's death."

Pierce leans back in his chair and nods.

"I've heard talk about their deal from the townsfolk."

Jeremy turns around and grins.

"On the subject of talk—seems you and Gina Bentley have been getting cozy lately. Should I plan a winter wedding?"

Pierce shakes his fist at Jeremy.

"Don't you start on me about Gina Bentley—we're just good friends and nothing more. She was there for me when my marriage hit the skids. But that's it—dead end. Case closed."

Jeremy wags his finger at Pierce.

Page **50**

"You could do a lot worse. Gina Bentley has seen you from every angle. I think the two of you are a matched pair."

"Enough already—I'm out of here."

Jeremy watches Pierce walk to the door.

"A man needs someone at night."

Pierce reaches for the doorknob and turns around.

8

Alan McGyver looks at the newspaper in his hand and sighs loudly as his eyes cloud over. He slowly stands up.

"It's been such a long time."

He looks around the hotel room.

"This will be quite a homecoming no doubt."

He walks to the kitchenette nearby.

"I wonder if that old house is still standing at Point Blye."

He grabs his cell phone and seems nervous.

9

"I don't see why I can't go out with him."

Katrina Kane glares at her father as he walks past her. She looks at the cell phone in her hand. As Eddie Kane turns around he sighs loudly. They stare at each other for a few seconds.

"He's bad news. You can do better."

Katrina rolls her eyes.

"I should've stayed in Europe. I can't believe you're acting this way. Lyle Lincoln is a nice guy. Why don't you like him?"

Eddie runs his fingers through his hair.

"That boy hangs with the wrong crowd. People talk and none of it is good. He got a girl pregnant last year. Like I said, you can do better—someone that respects you—a nice guy."

Katrina gestures with her hand. She waves her hand in the air and points at her father. She watches his reaction.

"Ugh—nice guys are boring—no game."

Eddie gives Katrina a cautious look and grimaces.

Page **51**

"This discussion is going nowhere. Tell that boy you can't meet him in Paradise Point—not today—not tomorrow—not ever as far as I'm concerned. He's off limits. There, I said it."

Katrina looks at Eddie with contempt.

"You're not the boss of me—I'm going out with Lyle and there's nothing you can do about it. I don't take orders."

Eddie grabs Katrina by the arm.

"I forbid it. That loser has only one thing on his mind and one thing only. I know exactly what he wants to do with you."

Katrina jerks free of his grip.

"*Ugh*—don't go there. What do you know about sex anyway—old people don't know how to have fun. *Ugh*—gross."

Eddie looks at his cell phone as it begins blinking.

"This conversation isn't over yet."

He walks to the door and stops.

"Stay away from Lyle Lincoln or else."

Katrina watches as Eddie leaves the room. She turns around and faces a huge mirror a few feet away. She grins.

"He can't stop me from seeing Lyle."

She begins dialing and smirks as Lyle answers.

10

Alice Banning shuts the door to her car and begins walking across the parking lot. As she walks, she realizes Laura McFee is following her. Alice stops and turns around to face Laura.

"What's your problem?"

Laura grins broadly.

"Stay away from Matt. Leave him be."

Alice licks her lips several times.

"What if I don't?"

Laura makes a slashing gesture with her hand.

"Things happen every day in small towns. People wind up dead. Sometimes people disappear. Whores especially can find themselves in really dangerous situations—scary actually."

Alice looks at Laura curiously.

Page 52

"Is that your way of threatening me?"

She takes a step forward.

"Because if it is—I think you should know I won't be told who I can and can't sleep with—especially by the likes of you."

Laura angrily clenches her fist.

"I'm warning you *bitch*—stay away from Matt—or things will get really scary for you. I've had it with you trying to bed my man—go find someone else—start at the local prison—there a lot of guys there without girlfriends to tend to their needs."

Alice makes a lewd gesture with her finger.

"Matt understands me—knows what I like in bed—has a way with his tongue—knows how to work his dick inside me."

Laura slaps Alice.

"There will be no more warnings."

Alice rubs her face and glares at Laura.

"You'll pay for that."

Laura grins.

"We'll see."

She turns to leave.

11

"You're a danger to good girls everywhere."

Melissa Marshall smiles slyly as she winks at Carter Willington and lets her finger slide across his penis. He grins.

"I warned you I wasn't to be trifled with."

He laughs and pulls her toward him.

"Made it clear you would come to depend on me."

Melissa reaches out to kiss him.

"You don't play fair."

Carter smirks knowingly.

"It is what it is—I won't apologize."

They kiss again. She gives Carter a knowing look.

"I need you to do something."

Carter looks at Melissa curiously.

"I'm not going to beat up my brother for you."

Melissa rolls her eyes and seems annoyed.

"Forget your brother—he'll get what's coming to him after what he did—I have something else in mind for you to do."

She strokes her lips seductively.

"I want you to seduce Marla Sherwood. Turn her into one of your girls. Teach her a lesson for being so goody-goody."

Carter makes a lewd gesture with his finger.

"Oh-oh—what happened between you two last week to cause you to want me to make a play for the town virgin?"

Melissa gestures with her hand.

"That bitch thinks she's all that and then some—touts the fact she's untouched—makes me and my friends look bad."

She grits her teeth.

"She told me to my face at Lyle's party that I was a whore. Said I was every guy's idea of a good time—insulted my rep."

Carter laughs loudly.

"Nothing she said was a lie—it's all true."

Melissa seems annoyed.

"I hate her—I'm going to teach that bitch a lesson she won't forget for insulting me. Losing her precious virginity to you will seal her fate—no longer will she be able to hold her purity over me and my friends. She'll be used goods—a lowly slut."

Carter glances at his penis.

"I'm up for the job—but that boyfriend of hers is in the way. He won't let me get anywhere near her—especially knowing the kind of guy I am—having had so many sexual partners."

Melissa jabs Carter.

"Fuck Christian Keller—he makes me sick. Since he began dating Marla he behaves like his family is scandal free. That jerk's brother has a worst rep than you—played around with his uncle's fat ugly wife two summers ago—split that marriage up."

She strokes her lips again.

"Hayden takes after his father's cousin. Jarod Keller was murdered several years back by a loon named Jennifer Parker. That chick was totally bats—killed a whole bunch of people. It was quite the story—everyone at first blamed Gina Bentley."

Carter sits up in bed.

"Isn't she the one who got her hands on a wad of cash and then used it to build that school for underprivileged kids?"

Melissa rolls her eyes again.

"Uh-huh—my cousin was friends with her. Told me the whole story last year when she visited from New York—said that it all started with a girl named Tiffany Johnson. Jennifer killed her and tried to frame Gina. Bodies kept turning up all over Marble Hills soon after and it took a while for the truth to come out."

Carter seems confused.

"I heard that Jennifer was actually Gina's half-sister but that Gina didn't know. There was also a bunch of stories about a dead girl coming back from the dead and torturing Gina."

Melissa wags her finger at Carter.

"I see you've been talking to Diane Gold."

Carter gestures with his hand.

"I hooked up with her two days ago. She blabbed it all to me—said she heard that Jennifer was killed by a ghost."

Melissa begins laughing.

"You need to stop listening to Diane—there are no such things as ghosts. Obviously people in Marble Hills have too much time on their hands. Seriously that story is as whacked as the story everyone in Salem tells about witches—ugh—small towns have the weirdest people—people with absolutely no lives."

Carter sits up in bed.

"Just because you don't believe in something doesn't make it not true—there were witnesses to some of those stories Diane told me about—one of which was a tough FBI guy."

Melissa jabs Carter again.

"I'll believe it when I see it myself."

She reaches out to stroke Carter's arm and sighs.

"I want Marla Sherwood in your bed by next week. I want that bitch put in her place—and when you're done with her you'll tell everyone you had her on your terms—soil her rep."

Carter grimaces.

"I'm not making any promises."

"I don't want a lousy promise—I want a guarantee. I want you to break her—once she's like the rest of us she'll have nowhere to turn but to me and my friends. I'll own that bitch."

Carter snaps his fingers.

"What's in it for me?"

Melissa grins slyly and licks her lips.

"You'll have the knowledge you popped her."

Carter seems pleased. He sighs.

12

Robert Campo sighs as he steps out of his car and slams the door shut. As he turns around he sees Riley Benson looking at him from a few feet away. He seems upset and gestures.

"What's going on? You look like hell."

Robert rolls his eyes.

"Ashley dumped me the other day."

Riley seems unimpressed.

"I told you she wouldn't play your game."

Robert seems annoyed.

"So what if I cheated—guys cheat on their girlfriends all the time. I'm a guy—I got horny and couldn't help it."

He sighs loudly.

"She said I was all wrong for her. Said I was a lousy boyfriend. She was in total bitch mode—really nasty."

Riley shakes his head.

"I warned you—Ashley isn't like some of the other girls you've played with—she won't tolerate you fooling around."

Robert runs his fingers through his hair.

"I want her back."

Riley laughs.

"Not gonna happen buddy."

He reaches out to pat Robert on his shoulder.

"You blew it."

He shakes his head.

"I think it's time for you to start mingling."

Page 56

Robert clenches his fist.

"So what if I slept with her friend behind her back. It was no big deal—why can't she just let it go? It meant nothing."

Riley looks at the street ahead and shrugs.

"Would you have been so forgiving if she had slept with one of your friends—was poked by someone you knew?"

Robert gives Riley a sharp look.

"If she slept with some dude behind my back or let one of my friends poke her then I'd be done with her—so over."

Riley sighs loudly.

"I think you just answered your question."

Robert clenches his fist angrily.

"Your rep isn't sparkling clean either."

Riley points his finger at Robert.

"I've never pretended to be boyfriend material."

He runs his fingers through his hair.

"Never promised to be faithful to a woman when I knew I was going to be bedding someone right after. I know my deal."

Robert and Riley look at each other.

13

"Uh-huh—I just saw them going at it. Laura must know that Alice is still lusting after her husband. It was something to see—Laura slapped Alice really hard—shouted at her that if she kept trying to bed her husband she'd have a nasty accident."

Diane Gold licks her lips as she looks at her cell phone and gestures with her hand. She seems to be enjoying herself.

"Laura looked like she could kill Alice."

Diane laughs.

"Uh-huh—if she had a gun she would have shot Alice Banning dead for sleeping with her husband. It would be quite the scene if something like that were to actually happen here."

She laughs again and nods.

"This town is so dull—nothing ever happens here—if Laura kills Alice I certainly wouldn't be upset—I'd do interviews."

She sighs loudly and looks at people walking by.

"Uh-huh—what do I care if someone like Alice Banning gets whacked by Laura McFee? She's nothing more than a trollop that can't leave decent married people alone. She's been around the block a couple of times—caused a few marriages to end up in a lawyer's office. Played doctor with my uncle too—got pregnant and aborted the child before he knew. She's a cheap trick."

She waves to a few people across the street.

"I've got to go—just saw a couple of friends heading to Springview. Bet there'll be some drama there really soon."

She laughs and shuts off her phone.

14

Charlene McColl smiles as she walks out of a store and begins walking across the lobby area of Springview Mall. She stops briefly to look down at her stomach. She's in the last months of pregnancy. From several feet away she hears her name being called and turns around to see Elizabeth coming toward her with Marvin at her side. She reaches out to hug Charlene.

"It's been a while since I've seen you. Hope everything is going well with your pregnancy. I bet Will is over the moon."

Charlene acknowledges Marvin.

"He can't wait—definitely a proud papa."

Charlene strokes her stomach.

"Just a couple more weeks and this baby will make its grand entrance and take control of our lives. I just hope I won't suck at being a mother—so much responsibility to adjust to."

Elizabeth nods in agreement.

"Having a baby is a life-changing experience but you'll do just fine. How can you fail with such a good man like Will at your side? He's something special no doubt—honest and loyal."

Charlene grins broadly again.

"I kissed quite few toads before I met him—but he was worth waiting for. He's been so supportive of me being pregnant and having mood swings throughout. I love him dearly."

Page 58

She glances at Marvin and winks slyly.

"When are you two going to make it official?"

Marvin grins and glances at Elizabeth with a knowing look.

"It's up to Elizabeth. I'm ready."

Elizabeth turns to look at Marvin curiously.

15

Gina Bentley looks at the rose in her hand as Pierce grins broadly while he closes the door behind him. He faces her.

"How are you doing?"

Gina looks at the rose again.

"I'm OK—just got a call."

Pierce seems confused and shrugs.

"Did someone call about Jennifer Parker again?"

Gina shakes her head and sighs again.

"It was Erin McHenry."

Pierce takes a step toward Gina.

"What did she want?"

Gina glances at her cell phone.

"She wants to meet me."

Pierce turns to look at Gina curiously.

"Did she say what for?"

Gina shakes her head again.

"Not really. Said something about wanting to know more about her father—said I could help her piece together parts of her life that was missing—that she never knew she had."

Pierce shoots Gina a cautious look.

"Erin McHenry has a checkered past—be careful."

Gina reaches out to pull Pierce toward her.

"I'll be on guard—I promise."

He kisses her.

"How's Eddie?"

Gina gives Pierce a knowing look.

"He's fine—but yeah, he's still not pleased that you and I have begun dating—he thinks you're a tad too old for me."

Pierce reaches out to stroke Gina's hair.

"I'm only twelve years older. Not exactly a candidate for a nursing home just yet. Still got plenty of game left in me."

Gina slides her arms around Pierce's waist.

"I know all about how much game you have—quite the dancer too—made me look bad when we went to your cousin's wedding last month. I had two left feet and it showed."

Pierce laughs.

"You were fine—no one cared."

He kisses her lightly.

"I'm happy—that's all that matters."

They look at each other.

"I'm sorry your marriage didn't work with Charlotte."

Pierce sighs loudly.

"We grew apart. It happens. I'm just glad you took it upon yourself to ask me out to dinner the day I got my divorce papers from Charlotte. I was such in a bad place that day—terrible."

Gina hugs Pierce warmly.

16

"My father isn't going to kill you if we have sex."

Katrina looks at Lyle Lincoln curiously as he runs his fingers through his hair nervously. She leans over to kiss him.

"He only said it to see how you'd react."

Lyle shakes his head.

"Uh-huh—I've heard plenty of stories about your dad. He was in a bunch of fights when he was younger—liked fighting."

Katrina pretends to slap Lyle.

"My dad grew up in an orphanage. He had to be tough to survive. But he's mellowed. Just relax already. You've got nothing to worry about Lyle. He knows how I feel about you. Knows he can't stop me from seeing you. Stop looking for excuses."

Lyle pulls away and sighs loudly.

"I like living—like being alive. I certainly wouldn't want to end up with your father pointing a gun at yours truly."

Katrina slyly slides her hands between Lyle's legs.

"Don't you want to take my virginity?"

Lyle grins broadly.

"What do you think?"

Katrina pulls Lyle toward her again.

"My dad won't lay a hand on you—I promise."

Lyle looks at Katrina nervously.

17

Kelvin Penney turns around to face Bruce Holland as they exit an elevator inside Springview Mall. He sighs loudly.

"I heard there's a new girl at **Martha Mitchell** High School according to Diane Gold. Said she just transferred from Bar Harbor. Diane said she thinks she's better than everyone else. Her father just got a job at some top law firm here in town."

Bruce rolls his eyes.

"Uh-huh—so says Diane. That bitch lies about everyone behind their back. I bet the new girl is sweet and innocent."

Kelvin gestures with his hand.

"I bet her pop is gonna be watching her like a hawk."

Bruce grins broadly.

"So what if he's the new top lawyer in town. I'm still gonna try and score. See if she'll put out—give me a wicked thrill."

Kelvin grimaces and shakes his fist.

"Do you want to place bets to see who can score with her first? Loser will have to go down low on Alison Brewster."

Bruce seems horrified and sighs.

"Ugh—you're sick Penney—but I'll take your dare. Hope you can stomach positioning yourself between Alison's legs."

He begins laughing. Kelvin makes a lewd gesture with his finger and jabs Bruce. He gestures wildly with his hand.

"It's you that will have to do the unthinkable with dear Alison. My rep speaks for itself. I don't lay down with dogs."

Bruce laughs loudly and points.

"I guess you forgot about Cassie Menzies."

Page **61**

Kelvin shakes his fist at Bruce.

"I never did her. I passed out and she made up what she said happened between us. Besides, Cassie lives in Castle Beach so she doesn't count. Only girls from Marble Hills are part of our deal—girls from other towns don't count—especially ones that can easily break a full-length mirror with just one glance."

Bruce wags his finger at Kelvin.

"So says you."

Kelvin stops and faces Bruce.

"I still haven't forgotten what happened between you and my sister. You treated her like trash—used and dumped her."

Bruce digs his hands into the front pockets of his Levi's as he looks toward where several girls are talking. He shrugs.

"Eden and I were never serious. We had sex—but I never promised her anything—she knew I was seeing other girls."

Kelvin seems irritated by the comment.

18

Will McColl watches as Charlene comes toward him from the front door of his office. He stands up and grins broadly.

"How have you been?"

Charlene looks down at her stomach.

"Just fine—our little surprise has been quite silent all day long. Must be gearing up for a party tonight—lots of action."

Will comes toward Charlene and slides his fingers across her protruding stomach and seems pleased. He kisses her.

"Just for the record so it can be known. I'm not sorry for putting a baby inside you—not sorry at all—enjoyed doing it."

"Is that so? What if I tell my brother?"

Will gleefully shrugs and then gently strokes Charlene's stomach for a few seconds as he kisses her again. He winks.

"I can't wait—can't wait to be a father."

Charlene touches Will's cheek and seems about to cry. Will notices and looks at her curiously. She wipes a tear away.

"You've just been so incredibly wonderful."

Will laughs and hugs Charlene.

"I owe it all to you."

They kiss again as he glances at Charlene's stomach once more before facing the office again. He gestures with his hand.

"From the moment you set your eye on me the day we met I've had it easy—I didn't have to do anything—you liked me for who I was and not who you could make me become."

Charlene touches his cheek again.

"I'm glad you and my brother are so tight."

Will gives Charlene a knowing look and winks.

"He warned me about you."

Charlene seems bothered and sighs.

"How dare he? Spill your guts husband of mine."

Will begins laughing as he pulls away from Charlene and looks at the front door briefly. She jabs him several times.

"What trash did Maxwell lay on you?"

Will wags his finger at Charlene.

"He said you were tough as nails and not to treat you like a delicate flower—said you wouldn't like being treated like that."

Charlene takes a step toward Will.

"I guess my brother knows me better than I thought."

She jabs Will yet again.

"What else did Maxwell say about me?"

Will back away and laughs.

"I think I should shut up right about now or my life could be in danger. I've seen how angry you can get—scary."

Charlene points her finger at Will. She watches as he glances at the front door. She takes a step toward him.

"What else did Maxwell say?"

She watches his reaction and sighs.

19

Diane steps off the elevator and sees Kelvin and Bruce standing several yards away. She walks over toward them.

"What are you two misfits up to?"

Kelvin waves his hand in the air.

"Don't you have somewhere else to be?"

Diane reacts and wags her finger at Kelvin and laughs.

"You two don't stand a chance with Jayne Gyston. She has too much class to be played by either of you—such losers."

Bruce makes a lewd gesture with his finger.

"So says the girl who got charmed by yours truly."

Diane looks at Bruce with disdain.

"I was drunk and you took advantage of me the night of Lyle's party. I don't even remember how bad you were."

Bruce begins laughing.

"Uh-huh—keep telling yourself that."

He looks at Kelvin.

"I was her first—took her because I could."

Diane seems ready to slap Bruce as she notices Liza Marshall talking to someone she can't see clearly. She faces Bruce and then walks away without another word. He laughs.

"Gave it up to me thinking we had a future."

He faces Kelvin and grins broadly.

"She wasn't any good in case you were wondering. I've had better. It was like fucking a corpse. Ugh—never again."

Kelvin rolls his eyes knowingly and shrugs.

"Doesn't matter if you poked her or not—she's much too icky for me to ever think about in that way—she's poison."

He laughs as he reaches out to jab Bruce.

"Whatever—but this deal we made about Alison is real nevertheless—you'll have no choice but to pleasure dear sweet Alison when I get Jayne Gyston between my legs and score."

Bruce seems upset and glances at Diane standing in a distance talking with Liza. He faces Kelvin again and sighs.

20

Robert looks at Diane and seems angry. He sighs.

"This was a private conversation."

Diane ignores him and faces Liza again.

Page 64

"You know how I feel about cheaters. This one here has loose morals. He'll use you just like he used Ashley. Plays like there's no need to be faithful—uses girls like tissue paper."

Robert clenches his fist.

"Don't you have somewhere else to be Diane?"

She faces him.

"I could say the same about you."

Robert gives Liza a sharp look and shrugs.

"She's raining on our parade."

Liza watches Diane's reaction.

"I'm good—I know his game—but I appreciate your concern. I'll be OK. I'll talk to you later. Call me in an hour."

Diane looks at Robert coldly and then Liza.

21

"Uh-huh—I miss Bar Harbor no doubt. But I'll adjust. It's not like I can't still hang out with my friends when I want to."

Jayne Gyston leans back in her chair and glances at the open window in her bedroom. She faces the computer again and glances at the screen as her mother looks back at her.

"I love you."

Wanda Gyston wipes a tear from her eye.

"I'm sorry that I can't leave Bar Harbor until my house arrest is completed. Damn your father for what he did."

Jayne sighs loudly.

"Daddy didn't do anything. You did it all to yourself mother. You tried to bribe a judge after you got arrested."

Wanda seems annoyed.

"I wouldn't have had to resort to such behavior if your father hadn't exposed me. He didn't have to tell Jamie Mazek that I was selling drugs to your friends. He could've ignored it."

Jayne gestures with her hand.

"I don't blame Daddy for anything."

Wanda seems stung by the words and shrugs.

"I didn't do anything wrong."

Jayne gives her mother a knowing look and glances at her cell phone as it begins to flash several times. She sighs.

"I've got to go mother. I'll talk to you later."

Wanda nods and the screen goes blank. Jayne turns to look at her cell phone and seems confused. She picks it up.

22

Trey Holder leans over and kisses Alice as she glances at his erection straining against his Lycra shorts. He laughs.

"It's been a while."

She rolls her eyes and smirks.

"It's been two days."

He laughs loudly and kisses her again.

"Two days is a long time—I'm horny—deal already."

She kisses him again.

"You're insatiable—shameless."

He nods and pulls his Lycra shorts down.

"I'm trapped in a loveless marriage."

He watches her reaction as his penis comes into view.

"I want to fuck all the time."

Alice reaches out to stroke his penis.

"You men are all the same—you want the women in your lives to spread their legs constantly. Give it up like candy."

Trey makes a lewd gesture with his finger.

"Excuse me for being a man."

He grabs her and they kiss passionately.

"I'm thinking of asking Carissa for a divorce."

Alice pulls away from Trey.

"What does that have to do with me?"

Trey shrugs.

"Nothing—I just thought you'd like to know I'll be a free man soon—no longer shackled to a frigid wife. No more sneaking around to get laid so I can keep my sanity—free to be me."

Alice seems confused and shakes her head.

"I thought you told me Carissa refused to let you go."

Page 66

"She did. She told me endless times we were married until death did us part—but that was before—before I tell her how much of a dog I've been. How much I've strayed and played."

He grins slyly and points to his penis.

"I intend to let her know that I've been poking every woman I found attractive—got two pregnant as well."

Alice looks at Trey curiously.

"You have children?"

Trey shakes his head.

"They aborted it. I'm free and clear."

He laughs loudly.

"But I intend to use that angle to send Carissa packing. If she thinks I slyly fathered two illegitimate children outside the confines of our marriage she'll kick me to the curb instantly—and I'll be free to live my life the way I want to. She'll drop me the minute she thinks I have two bastard children to tend to."

Alice wags her finger at Trey.

"Don't you tell Carissa about the two of us—I don't want your wife trash-talking my name all over this wretched town."

Trey gives Alice a knowing look.

TO BE CONTINUED

A Brief Look at the Third Episode

Townspeople play with fire as lives begin unraveling when secrets come out about several couples in Marble Hills—while someone goes too far pursuing revenge in order to even an old score.

Episode 3
Perfect Image

1

"He's been cheating on me—I know that for a fact."

Carissa Holder slowly turns around to face her friend and sighs loudly. Nola French reaches out to touch Carissa's shoulder as they look at each other. Carissa seems visibly upset.

"He promised me—said he'd be true."

Nola laughs.

"This is Trey Holder we're talking about—he's always been a player—strayed plenty with every girl in town. He's a user."

Carissa clenches her fist.

"Have you heard something?"

Nola shrugs.

"I try not to listen to meaningless gossip."

Carissa seems annoyed.

"That isn't an answer."

Nola glances at her cell phone flashing.

"People in this town talk—most of the time what you hear is not what really happened—embellished quite a bit by the time it comes full circle. Marble Hills is quite dull mostly."

Page **69**

Carissa shakes her fist at Nola and sighs.

"I swear if Trey's been dipping his wick around town I'll teach him—make him pay for fooling around behind my back."

Nola faces Carissa.

"What are you gonna do?"

Carissa grins slyly.

"I'm not sure yet—but Trey better watch his step if he knows what's good for him. Things happen—really bad things have happened to husbands who lie to their wives—and if he's done anything to shame me I'll make sure he feels my wrath."

Nola reacts.

"Murder will get you life."

Carissa waves her hand in the air.

2

Will McColl looks up as Eddie Kane closes the front door of the police station behind him. He turns to face Will and sighs.

"Where's your deputy?"

Will gestures with his hand.

"Out—should be back in several hours."

Eddie grimaces.

"Uh-huh—I'll just bet. Seems he spends most of his time chasing women all over town. Keeps him quite busy if truth be known—I think it's time you think of replacing that loser."

Will leans forward.

"No one else wants the job."

Eddie wags his finger at Will and smirks.

"I'll keep my eyes open. I'm sure we can find someone who isn't always trolling social media for potential dates."

Will nods and gives Eddie a knowing look.

"What brings you here today?"

Eddie shrugs.

"It appears my dear father—who shall remain forever nameless—has left several more surprises after the fact."

Will seems confused and sighs loudly.

Page **70**

"But I thought David Sawyer was the last piece of the puzzle that Carmen Pendleton alluded to initially that day at Glass Owl? His true parentage caused quite a gossipy stir when it was revealed that not only was he Brad McKinley's biological brother—but that they were both the sons of "he who shall remain nameless" making them your half-brothers as well."

Eddie grimaces again and seems irritated.

"Finding out David Sawyer was my half-brother was a shock—but he's a good kid—nothing like his rotten twin—he and I have gotten to know each other quite well—got no problem with him being my brother—but this Alec Martel person could be a whole different story. Seems he thinks he's my half-brother too based on some notation in his mother's diary. No doubt he wants a chunk of the estate for himself—what's left of it anyway."

Will glances at Eddie nervously.

"I thought most of the estate went to fund the education center as part of the deal with Gina Bentley way back when?"

Eddie clenches his fist.

"It did—but this new twist with Martel could really cause a few wrinkles in the deal. I have to find out what's his game."

"I assume you have people on it already."

Eddie grins slyly.

"Uh-huh—right now as we speak Martel's family is being checked out by my top people in Bermuda—no stone will be left unturned—if he is who he says he is—I'll deal with it—but not before I know for sure. He seems by all accounts to be willing to do anything to get what he wants—no scheme is too complicated for someone desperate to get their hands on a ton of cash."

"Bermuda—man, your pop got around."

Eddie spins around to face Will.

"Don't ever call that wretched excuse my father. My *father* died in an explosion with my mother when I was a kid. He's my *real* father—my only father as far as I'm concerned—I've never needed or wanted anyone else—not then—and not now."

Will reacts to Eddie's anger.

"I didn't mean anything by it."

Eddie wags his finger at Will.

"I know you didn't."

He glances at the front door and sighs.

"I'm still dealing with everything I found out that day at Glass Owl—nothing has been the same since. My life was turned upside down with what Carmen Pendleton told me."

Will sighs and nods in agreement.

3

"Uh-huh—that's right Marilyn, it's been a long time coming. But I have to do it—got to find out the truth—ease my conscious. If that house comes down before I find out what really happened when I was twelve—there will be no way to ever clear my name—or make sense of what happened decades ago."

Alan McGyver seems irritated.

"Of course I know what this will look like if the police find out what happened before I talk to those involved."

He angrily grits his teeth.

"But I'm gonna right a wrong regardless—case closed."

He sighs loudly and waves his hand in the air.

"Don't worry about me or what I'm gonna do. I won't let this slide like what happened in the **Irene Garza** case from 1960. It took over fifty years for justice to be dealt and still the law failed her. Her frigging killer almost got away with murder."

He nods several times.

"I'm gonna make sure what happened is dealt with."

He waves his hand in the air again and sighs.

"It'll just be a matter of time before the right moment presents itself. I'll right the wrong that was done concerning what took place at that old house—it's the least I can do after all these years of wondering and not knowing for sure exactly if I was somehow responsible for the death of another human being."

He clenches his fist and looks at his cell phone.

"No one will blame me for doing what I have planned if it was their relative that was killed and the truth hushed up."

Page 72

He glances at a newspaper lying on the coffee table not far away from the sofa. He runs his fingers through his hair.

"I'll take your concern into consideration."

He nods again as he picks up the newspaper.

4

"I don't know—she's not my type."

Robert Campo looks at Malcolm Kemp with disgust.

"Look, I'm not asking you to go out on a date with that miserable bitch. I'm just asking you to fuck her—play her."

He laughs loudly.

"Diane Gold needs to know who's really in charge in this town. She thinks she can change the topic of conversations with her malicious gossip—I'm so sick of hearing her babble."

Malcolm wrings his hands.

"What if she cries rape?"

Robert makes a lewd gesture with his finger.

"How can she? You and Diane will fuck in the backseat of your car after pretending you want to date her. Once you've had her—you'll dump her right after—make her feel like trash."

Robert shoves Malcolm.

"Seriously, you've been having a dry spell since you split with Amanda Zyperton. It's time for you to get back on the horse and bag another stupid Plain Jane chick. Diane is perfect."

Malcolm shakes his head.

"She doesn't dig me—ignores me all the time."

Robert grins slyly.

"I've got a plan to remedy that."

Malcolm looks at Robert curiously.

"I don't want to be a part of some whacked scheme that you and your friends will come up with. I haven't forgotten what happened with Marcia last year. She was totally devastated."

Robert makes a lewd gesture with his finger again.

"Marcia Wynton is a dog. She deserved what my friends and I did to her. She lost her virginity to three horny guys."

Page **73**

Robert knowingly wags his finger at Malcolm.

"Marcia got poked by me and my friends—fun was had by all—OK. End of story. Each of us got something sweet."

Malcolm looks at Robert curiously.

"Uh-huh—she claimed she was raped."

Robert rolls his eyes knowingly.

"Of course she'd say that. What would you say if you got played by a bunch of guys looking for a good time?"

Malcolm seems uneasy.

"OK—whatever. Nevertheless Diane and I aren't going to happen. She thinks I'm a dweeb. She likes dumb jocks."

Robert snaps his fingers in front of Malcolm's face.

"Let me worry about that."

He glances at his cell phone.

"One call is all it'll take."

Malcolm runs his fingers through his hair.

"I don't know about this. Your plans always seem to end up with someone else getting blamed for your schemes."

Robert gestures at Malcolm.

"Says who?"

Malcolm rolls his eyes.

5

Steve Pendleton sighs as he watches his son walk towards him on the pier. Several seagulls drop lazily into the sea as Taylor Pendleton gives his father a strange look. He seems upset.

"How's mom?"

Steve leans against the wooden pier.

"How should I know?"

Taylor digs his hands into the front pocket of his jeans.

"You've got to end it with her—today."

Steve sighs loudly.

"What are you talking about?"

Taylor glances at the waves in a distance.

"Yvette Vanderpoole."

Steve seems annoyed and shrugs.

"I don't know what you're talking about."

Taylor reaches out and grabs his father by the arm.

"She and you—she's not very good at keeping secrets with guys she sleeps with. She told me about the two of you."

Steve turns to face Taylor.

"Yvette lies. There's nothing going on between us. We're just really good friends, OK—nothing more than that."

Taylor takes a step toward his father.

"Uh-huh—I know the truth about you pops. You've been a player all your life. I've heard plenty. It's time to come clean."

Steve suddenly seems enraged.

"I think you should take a page out of your own book before you point fingers at your dear old dad. You have a rep around Marble Hills—Paradise Point too from what I've heard. You've sowed plenty of wild oats lately with several girls—took some of them to an abortion clinic a few times if I recall."

Taylor makes a lewd gesture with his finger.

"So what—I'm a single guy—I can fuck whomever I feel like sleeping with at any particular moment. But you—you're a married man—married to my mother—you're a father."

Steve grabs Taylor by the collar.

"Your mother and I have had our issues. Mind your own damn business is you know what's good for you. Zip it."

Taylor jerks free of Steve's grasp.

"Fuck you."

He looks at his father one last time and storms off. Steve watches him go and seems about to explode. He sighs.

"The nerve of that boy for telling me how to live my life after all the trouble he's been in since he turned eighteen."

He clenches his fist.

"I might have to teach him a lesson."

He clenches his fist again.

"One he won't forget for years to come. Damn him for trying my last nerve today—maybe it's time I taught that foolish son of mine how life really works—inflict plenty of pain."

He watches as Taylor drives off in a jeep and grimaces.

"Where did I go wrong with that boy?"

He reaches for his cell phone and begins dialing.

<h1 style="text-align:center">6</h1>

<h2 style="text-align:center">Paradise Point</h2>

Katrina Kane seems upset as Lyle Lincoln stops to look at waves crashing on rocks a few feet away. She reaches for his hand and pulls him toward her. She grins slyly and sighs.

"I want to give myself to you."

Katrina slides her fingers across Lyle's lips.

"You're my boyfriend—you'll have to take me sooner or later in the backseat of your car—make me a woman—make sure everyone in town knows I'm your girl—knows you took me."

Lyle turns to look at Katrina and grins.

"This could end badly."

Katrina seems irritated and shrugs.

"Enough about my dad—he won't rub you out if you free me of my virginity. He knows how I feel about you."

Lyle pulls Katrina toward him.

"I'm not a fighter."

Katrina gives Lyle a knowing look.

"I can handle my father."

She looks at the buttons on his Levi's and licks her lips.

"I'm not the type of girl that tolerates wimps."

Lyle seems uneasy.

"How about we go up the coast?"

Katrina smiles broadly.

"I'm game if you intend to make your move on me."

Lyle turns away.

"If I lose my life at the hands of your deranged father it'll be your fault that I'm sleeping six feet under a pile of dirt."

Katrina playfully slaps Lyle.

"My father's not deranged Lyle. He just knows how guys think and what they want—he was wild when he was young."

Page 76

"Uh-huh—so you tell me all the time—but I think your father was never a kid—just a really pissed off adult."

Katrina playfully slaps Lyle again.

7

Matt McFee grins as he watches Marla Jefferson eagerly tugging at his boxer briefs. Her fingers slowly trace his massive erection underneath as she looks up at him. He grins broadly.

"Laura is on the warpath again."

Marla rolls her eyes.

"That wife of yours is seriously crimping your style."

Matt nods in agreement.

"Tell me something I don't know."

He watches as she slowly pulls his underwear down and begins stroking his penis as it juts out at her. She sighs loudly.

"I bet Laura hates how tight your pants are?"

Matt laughs and gestures with his hand.

"Uh-huh—she thinks I'm trying to get Alice's attention when I go jogging. But she's wrong on that idea—so wrong."

He watches as she mouths his penis.

"I've got my eye elsewhere."

He moans loudly seconds later.

"No one gives blow like you."

He watches as she hastily swallows a load of semen as he begins coming again. He grins slyly and looks at his watch.

"I heard you and the hubby split for good?"

Matt gives Marla a knowing look.

"No spark left?"

Marla swallows again and stands up.

"He and I just had nothing left to talk about."

Matt winks at Marla.

"Did he know about us?"

Marla shrugs.

"If he did he never said anything."

She leans against Matt.

Page 77

"Since Lana died we've been drifting. It wasn't a surprise to anyone. Of course, like you said, Kent probably had inklings about the fact I've been seeing other guys—for years now."

She seems upset and sighs.

"Lana and I had our differences but I loved her. It all happened so suddenly that summer. Her murder is something I don't think I'll ever get over. That Parker girl caused so much pain in Marble Hills—and for what—to get even with one of her classmates for sleeping with her boyfriend—who later turned out to be her half-sister. It was all so crazy that it took me almost a year to face what actually happened to my daughter."

Matt tenderly puts his arms around Marla.

"I'm sorry about Lana."

Marla wipes a tear away.

"People still talk about it in Marble Hills. Still talks trash about my daughter's tragic fate—saying she was the town tramp and she deserved to be slaughtered by that unstable fiend."

Matt gives Marla a knowing look.

"Maybe you should move to out of town?"

Marla turns to face Matt.

"I've thought about it—certainly would make it easier for you and me to get together. Unless Laura handcuffs you to her bed and forbids you to leave the house—lays down the law."

Matt laughs loudly.

"She's not that bad. She just has a hard time dealing with the fact I've been promiscuous throughout our marriage."

He makes a lewd gesture with his finger.

"I've tried—I've really tried. But I just can't conform to her way of thinking. I need to have my own life—live a little."

Marla strokes Matt's cheek with her fingers and looks down at his penis sticking out in front of him. She smirks.

"I know that feeling all too well."

He glances slyly at the bed not far away in the sparsely decorated motel room. He gestures with his hand.

"I could use some extra attention right about now."

They kiss lightly and then more passionately.

Will leans back in his chair and looks at Eddie as he reaches for the doorknob. Will gestures with his hand.

"Have you heard from Kyle lately?"

Eddie shakes his head.

"He and Serena are happy in Sydney. Last I heard he said he wasn't planning on returning to the States anytime soon."

He points his finger at Will.

"Patrick came clean about what happened at Tolling Bell with Gary Glick. He got probation. Serena's younger brother Malcolm decided to stay in New England as you know. Lives in Castle Beach most of the year when he's not traveling—he's quite the artist with a brush and a piece of canvas—does the **Gilbert Stuart** thing really well—I've bought a few pieces myself."

Will rolls his eyes and laughs.

"Didn't figure you for liking art?"

Eddie takes a step forward.

"Lots of things you don't know about me McColl."

Will leans forward and grins broadly.

"Do tell—starting with what happened that day at Glass Owl. There's been plenty of talk about the weird goings-on while you were there that day—you and Todd Spencer have been quite tight-lipped about the mysterious details—time to spill."

Eddie wipes sweat from his brow.

"Nothing to tell—there was a suicide of which you know and then an incident involving a thug from Boston who gunned down reporters on the orders of Calvin Whitney's daughter."

Will stands up and sighs loudly.

"Actually I was talking about the incident involving Tiffany Johnson—of whom the education center is named after."

Eddie wipes his brow again.

"No story there—it never happened—nothing but tales about things that go bump in the night—Hollywood stuff."

Will walks over to where Eddie is standing.

"That's not what I heard."

Eddie waves his hand in the air.

"I don't know anything other than what I told you."

Will grimaces and jabs Eddie in the chest.

"Spencer's kid said he saw Tiffany Johnson that day at Glass Owl—said she was real as anything—lectured you guys."

Eddie begins laughing.

"Last thing you want to do is believe anything that Simon Spencer says. Kid graduated college with a degree in writing."

Eddie jabs Will and laughs.

"He's been pulling your leg for kicks. Todd said he's been working on his first novel. Something about a small New England town haunted by several murders—heard there's a ghost angle in the storyline. You got played for a fool by a twenty-two-year-old kid with relationship issues. Do yourself a favor and cut your losses while you're ahead—best for everyone involved."

Will glances at Eddie oddly.

"Simon wasn't the only one who told me about what happened that afternoon. I guess I'll have to dig deeper if I want to get to the truth—maybe I should start with Jason Anderson."

Eddie suddenly seems upset.

"Leave it be Will—Jason has been through a lot—just graduated with honors from Boston University. He doesn't need you meddling in the past because you like watching those shows on cable about houses with ghosts and other weird stuff."

Will turns away and sighs.

"Fine—whatever—you win this round."

Eddie grins broadly.

9

Trey Holder slams the door shut and walks into the kitchen as he sees Carissa looking at him with a cold stare.

"What now?"

Carissa walks toward Trey.

"I'm losing patience with your behavior."

Trey sighs loudly.

"I don't know what you're talking about."

Carissa clenches her fist.

"It's come to my attention that you were seen earlier leaving a hotel room with Alice Banning. Kissing and groping her breasts several times—forgetting you're a married man."

Trey begins laughing.

"Who's been telling you lies. I haven't seen Alice today or yesterday for that fact. I was at the park exercising."

Carissa walks toward Trey.

"Likely story—more like exercising with that whore at that sleazy hotel on Clark Avenue—the one that caters to hookers."

Trey laughs loudly.

"Uh-huh—that's right Carissa—go on—believe vicious lies from your friends about your faithful husband. No wonder we're having problems—with friends like yours you don't need enemies out there looking to destroy our marriage—fuck them."

Carissa grabs Trey by the arm.

"I'm not letting you off the hook that easy. I'll never leave you—never give you a divorce—never—do you hear me."

They look at each other intently for a few seconds before Trey jerks free of Carissa's grip and walks away. She sighs.

"I meant it Trey—I'll never let you go."

He turns around to look at her curiously.

10

Nola sits down at a table in a small diner and is about to pick up a menu when Alice Banning walks by. Nola sighs loudly.

"What some people won't do?"

Alice suddenly spins around and faces Nola.

"Excuse me."

Nola rolls her eyes.

"How's Matt?"

Alice reacts. She notices a few people staring at them as Nola seems to be enjoying the attention. Alice glares at her.

Page 81

"Better watch your damn mouth, *bitch*. No one likes a busybody—least of all in Marble Hills—you of all people."

Nola notices several people looking at them.

"Is there no man you won't fuck?"

Alice seems about to explode and then smirks slyly.

"Well, I won't fuck Frank again—used goods."

Nola suddenly stands up.

"You're a piece of trash—sleeping with every man you can get your clutches into. Frank and I had something special."

Alice makes a lewd gesture with her finger.

"Seems to me if it was so special he wouldn't have come asking me for some action on his anniversary of all days."

Nola picks up a glass of water and throws it at Alice.

"How dare you."

Several people begin to laugh.

"I'll get you for this—I'll make you pay."

Nola gestures with her hand.

"Bring it on—I'll break you."

Alice notices people staring at her and turns to leave in a rush. Claps begin slowly then become louder as Nola smiles.

11
Paradise Point

Katrina seductively looks at Lyle as her fingers slide across the buttons on his Levi's. He looks at her nervously and sighs.

"You know I want to make love to you."

Katrina pushes Lyle against his car.

"Well, why don't you make your move already? Show me how much you want me—make me one of your girls."

He sighs loudly.

"I like living."

Katrina rolls her eyes.

"I already told you—my father won't hurt you. He just needs to get to know you and then he'll be your biggest fan."

Lyle pulls away from Katrina.

"I've got a history. I've slept around a bit—most of the girls in this area of Maine and I know each other intimately."

Katrina rolls her eyes again.

"Duh—I already know about your history. So what if you're not a virgin anymore. I want to give myself to you anyway. I want you to be my first. Look, you're a nice guy—everyone in town likes you—no one has ever said a bad thing about you."

Lyle grins broadly.

"I *am* a nice guy—terribly horny maybe—but nice."

Katrina tousles Lyle's hair.

"How about we meet tomorrow at Pirate's Cove—find a deserted part of the beach—spread a plush blanket?"

Katrina notices Lyle's erection.

"I'll take that as a yes."

Lyle nods in agreement and laughs.

12

Steve downs another mug of beer as he notices Alice coming toward him at the dimly-lit bar. He grins broadly.

"Who pissed you off today?"

Alice sits down next to Steve.

"Nola French."

Steve rolls his eyes.

"Say no more."

Steve looks at the empty mug in front of him.

"How about I buy you a beer?"

Alice grins slyly.

"I'm game."

She leans closer toward Steve.

"That bitch made a scene at Sky's Diner earlier. Called me out for breaking up her marriage—it got really ugly."

Steve makes a lewd gesture with his finger and grins.

"I'll just bet. Nola isn't one to back away from a fight. She and Frank had it out plenty before he walked out on her."

Alice licks her lips seductively.

"He wasn't much in bed if truth be known."
She gives Steve a knowing look.
"He certainly didn't have the kind of spark you have."
Steve wags his finger at Alice.
"Not many guys do."
Alice slaps Steve gently.
"I see you haven't lost your huge ego since we split two months ago. You've probably been scoring left and right."
Steve begins laughing.
"I was playing even before we split."
Alice seems annoyed and shakes her hand at Steve.
"How does your wife put up with you?"
Steve sticks his finger into his mouth and gags.
"We have different goals."
Alice leans closer to Steve and winks.
"How about we blow this joint and head back to my place for a quick romp. I really need someone like you right now."
Steve pulls Alice toward him.
"Why did we split up in the first place?"
Alice seems upset.
"You slept with my sister."
Steve laughs loudly.
"Oh yeah—where is your sister anyway?"
Alice winces.
"That whore left town and moved in with my cousin from Castle Beach. Good riddance—she and I aren't speaking."
Steve laughs again.
"It was no big deal—your little sis just wanted to know what was so special about me and made a pass that I couldn't refuse. She even booked a swanky hotel room in advance."
Alice angrily jabs Steve.
"I hate her. I never want to see her again."
Steve winks slyly and glances at the front door.
"You and I really need to experience a moment together to relieve some serious tension. No strings attached."
Alice glances at Steve's bulging erection and grins.

Page 84

"I guess it can't hurt."

Steve makes a lewd gesture with his tongue.

"Unless you want to play it rough like we did on plenty of occasions back in the day—as I recall you always got really excited just before we fucked—made a point of letting me know my place as we got down to business—made me beg plenty."

Alice giggles as they walk toward the door.

13

Boothbay Harbor

Pierce Colby looks at the menu in front of him and then at Gina Bentley. He sighs loudly several times and seems upset.

"There's been a wrinkle concerning your father."

Gina seems confused.

"What has Erin McHenry done now?"

Pierce wipes sweat from his brow and grimaces.

"This isn't about the McHenry girl. It seems that someone in Bermuda has come forward recently claiming to be yet another Madison offspring. He's flying to Boston later this week."

Gina seems upset.

"I have another sibling?"

Pierce nods.

"It seems so. His name is Alec Martel. Grew up in Bermuda—still lives there from what I was told—seems nice."

Gina folds her hands in front of her.

"But Carmen Pendleton said there was no more siblings after David Sawyer came forward—said he was the last."

Pierce glances at his cell phone lying nearby.

"Apparently she was wrong. From what we know this dude has proof according to his lawyer. It appears legit."

Gina seems in shock.

"*We*—who's we?"

Pierce gives Gina a knowing look.

"Eddie."

He sighs loudly.

Page **85**

"He was told earlier today."

"What do we do?"

Pierce waves his hand in the air.

"I'm not sure. The ball is in Martel's court right now. If he asks for money we'll have to figure things out—and fast."

Gina gives Pierce a curious look.

14

"I told you she's not into me—I'm nothing to her."

Robert rolls his eyes as he pushes Malcolm through the sliding glass doors of a small cafe located inside a badly decorated movie theater that seems to be a throwback to the 1980s. In the corner they notice Diane Gold sitting by herself.

"This is doomed to end in failure."

Robert jabs Malcolm and pushes him again.

"I told you I have it all figured out where you and Diane are concerned. You and that bitch will end up in the backseat of her car where you'll show her how the game is really played."

Robert clenches his fist.

"You'll fuck her like the cheap slut she is and then tell her you just want to be friends. Tell her you're not into having anything serious right now. Her reaction will be priceless."

Malcolm nervously glances at Diane.

"This is cruel—even for someone like Diane."

Robert laughs.

"So what—that bitch needs to know exactly who's running things in this town—and reality check—it ain't her."

Robert jabs Malcolm once again.

"You'll be a legend when you're done with her. Girls will line up to be with you—simply because you dogged Diane."

They look at each other.

"I'm still not digging this idea."

Robert pushes Malcolm backwards.

"Don't fuck this up or I swear I'll make you wish you were never born—and you know I can do it too—my rep doesn't lie."

Page **86**

Malcolm backs away from Robert.

"What kind of person are you?"

Robert grins slyly and points at Diane.

"I'm the kind of guy who wants to make that wretched gossipy bitch beg for mercy after her reputation has been ruined by yours truly—I want to see her at a point of no return."

He begins laughing.

"Once she's been played I'll play her even further by pretending to like her—only until I bed her of course."

He winks at Malcolm.

"Uh-huh—I'll break her and take her to the brink—teach her a lesson for fucking around with me the way she did."

Malcolm looks over at Diane again.

"What if every girl in Marble Hills thinks I'm a douche if I treat Diane the way you say I should—I'll be like that guy—Arch Bennow—you know, the one who bedded his teacher the night of the junior prom—which caused his girlfriend to kill herself."

Robert grins broadly and laughs.

"Arch is a god—he did what every guy wants to do—fuck a hot teacher in front of his girlfriend. That stupid bitch didn't know how lucky she was to be Arch's girlfriend. He's my hero."

Malcolm shakes his head.

"Where is he? I haven't seen him in a while?"

Robert smirks and slaps Malcolm lightly on the back.

"Dude is attending college in New York. Heard he got two girls pregnant first month he got there—he's such a rebel."

Malcolm looks at Robert curiously.

15

"Some things are never what they seem."

Todd Spencer takes a swig of beer as he looks at Eddie sitting next to him with a knowing look at an outdoor bar.

"Who knew that your pop had another kid out there that no one knew about? Plays like an episode of *Falcon Crest*."

Eddie jabs Todd. He seems upset.

Page **87**

"I told you never to call that creep my father. Bastard is still causing trouble despite being dead for several years now."

Todd gestures with his hand.

"What does this guy want—a bag of money?"

Eddie shrugs and takes a sip of his beer.

"I'm not sure yet—don't even know what he looks like."

Todd rolls his eyes.

"Duh—Google him and find out—everybody has a profile nowadays. Bet you anything he wants his share of the loot."

Eddie shoves Todd gently.

"Don't you think I did that already? Alec Martel doesn't have a profile—no social media info whatsoever—blank."

Todd shoots Eddie a worried look.

"Maybe he's using the name Madison?"

Eddie shakes his fist at Todd.

"There's nothing under Madison either. This guy is not into having people know anything about him—he probably has a whole list of issues he's dealing with—royally messed up."

Eddie takes another sip of beer.

"And if this unraveling Martel situation isn't enough to deal with at the moment—it seems that Will McColl thinks he's one of the *Hardy Boys*—he was aggressively digging for info earlier about what happened that day at Glass Owl—asking all sorts of trigger questions about Tiffany Johnson—wanting to know details on what really took place—kept badgering."

Todd suddenly seems upset.

"You didn't tell him what we saw did you?"

Eddie gives Todd an odd look.

"Do I look stupid? Of course I didn't tell him what we saw and about what happened. If he knew about the info Tiffany Johnson bestowed on us that day, he'd freak. Like seriously, even now I can't explain what happened to us that afternoon at Glass Owl. Having a dead teenager tell us that we were all there at that moment for a reason—and that when the time came we'd know what had to be done. It would freak any sane person out."

Todd wipes sweat from his brow and gestures briefly.

"Have you seen Tiffany Johnson since?"

Eddie seems about to laugh.

"No—have you?"

Todd shakes his head and looks around at several of the other patrons at the bar. He faces Eddie again and sighs.

"I wonder if Simon has seen her."

Eddie shoots Todd a warning look.

"Don't go there—leave sleeping dogs lie."

Todd takes a swig of beer again.

"Sort of weird dealing with my adult son now—he's so mature—filled with a sense of duty—talks like he's my father."

Eddie snickers and points.

"I already got that problem with Katrina. She knows more than I do—and not afraid to tell me so either whenever I piss her off. She's sixteen going on forty—now I know how **Otto Frank** felt when he read his late daughter's diary. From what I heard he came to realize she was more of an adult than he was. But yet he must have been so proud. **Anne Frank** changed history."

Todd runs his fingers through his hair.

"I second that. Her diary is the second highest selling work of nonfiction next to the Bible. Quite an accomplishment for a teenager who never thought people would care about what she had to say in her handwritten diary. To this day you can't walk by a bookstore that doesn't have a printed copy in the window."

Eddie shakes his head and seems upset.

"I don't know what I'd do if something happened to my girls—they're my reason for being—they give me purpose."

Todd reaches out to pat Eddie on the shoulder.

"Uh-huh—I knew beneath all that bluster you were a total creampuff at heart. Fatherhood has made you a wimp."

Eddie playfully grabs Todd by the collar.

"I can still easily belt you if I had to."

He lets go of Todd.

"I'm putty in their hands."

Todd grins and takes another swig.

"They know it too."

Eddie glances at his cell phone. He sighs loudly.

"Katrina has been seeing a local teenage punk. He's the nephew of Ben Lincoln who taught for a while here a few years back. She hangs on his every word—makes me sick to think my little girl being around some horny young man with only one thing on his mind—makes me crazy enough to hurt him."

Todd wags his finger at Eddie.

"I've been through that game already with Simon. He hung around girls at college with questionable reputations but he turned out fine nevertheless. He's been seeing the same girl for the last year or so—never asks for advice from his dear old father even though I constantly offer my knowledge about life."

Eddie seems bothered and shrugs.

"Maybe there's still hope with Laurel."

Todd rolls his eyes at Eddie.

"Has she discovered boys yet?"

Eddie grimaces.

"She's fourteen—what do you think?"

He reaches for his mug of beer nearby and sighs.

16
Paradise Point

Simone Holland watches as Kent Jefferson pulls a chair out for her. He smiles as she sits down at a dimly-lit table.

"You didn't have to go that extra mile."

Kent waves his hand.

"Old habits are hard to break."

He sits down at the table and shrugs.

"It's been a while since I went on a date—married most of my life to the same woman—until it ended—things change."

"You're a sweet man."

Kent sighs and manages a smile.

"I hope you don't think I'm a weirdo for wanting to have our first dinner in Paradise Point and not Marble Hills."

Simone gives Kent a knowing look.

"I'm aware of the gossip that permeates Marble Hills on any given day. People ought to get a life instead of minding what other people might be doing behind closed doors."

Kent nods in agreement.

"My life has been in shambles since Marla and I split not long ago. But then again losing Lana changed everything."

Simone reacts and leans toward Kent.

"I'm really sorry about Lana. I didn't know her that well but she seemed like a sweet girl to me whenever we'd talk."

Kent nods and picks up a menu nearby.

"She was the light of my life. Losing her really changed how I see life. I don't take anything for granted anymore."

Simone notices several people she knows and waves before facing Kent again. She gestures with her hand.

"I could only imagine your pain."

Kent slowly wipes sweat from his brow.

"I got a call from a film producer yesterday."

Simone looks at Kent curiously.

"What did they want?"

Kent looks around at the small diner.

"He wanted to know if I wanted to help him make a movie about what happened to my daughter and the others."

Simone reacts and seems bothered.

"I thought the movie deal was shelved when Gina Bentley dropped out of the project? I heard there were some other deals pending but assumed they had fallen through as well."

Kent lowers his voice.

"That was my impression too but apparently Netflix still wants to turn what happened in Marble Hills into a movie."

Simone glances at the menu in her hand.

"I guess Hollywood just doesn't know when to leave well enough alone concerning exploitation. That said I've seen some of the movies Netflix have made—they're not bad actually."

Kent gestures with his hand.

"Doesn't matter anyway—I told them no."

Simone nods in agreement and sighs loudly.

17

"What if I get pregnant? What would you do?"

Elizabeth Pendleton looks at Marvin Houston curiously as he shrugs and smirks. She drops an empty box of condoms into the trash. He laughs and pulls her toward him with a smirk.

"I guess I should've picked up a fresh box of condoms before I came home? Oh well, I'll do it first thing tomorrow."

He gives her a sly look.

"In the meantime you and I need to get busy."

Elizabeth pushes him away.

"It ain't happening."

He seems disappointed and laughs.

"But I'm in the mood?"

Elizabeth walks toward the kitchen as Marvin follows. He reaches out to grab her again. They kiss passionately.

"I could go over to the drugstore?"

Elizabeth smiles and glances at the door.

"I'll be waiting."

Marvin looks at Elizabeth again and heads to the door. He stops suddenly and faces her. He gestures with his hand.

"For the record I don't see the point."

Elizabeth points to the door.

"I do."

He sighs.

"If my mother calls, tell her I'll call her back."

Elizabeth nods and watches him go.

"I'm so lucky to have found someone like him."

She sighs loudly and continues walking into the kitchen just as her cell phone begins ringing. She grabs it and reacts.

"What does *he* want?"

She looks at the name displayed on the phone again and pauses for a second or two before answering it. She shrugs.

"I thought I told you not to call me anymore."

She nods several times and turns to face the door.

"I already told you I can't help you Adrian. This is your mess to clean up. Why don't you call Marla Jefferson? I'm sure she'll be more than happy to hear from you now that you've been sprung from jail for selling drugs to students at **Nancy Hanks Lincoln** High School in Paradise Point. Go ahead, call her."

She walks toward the balcony and grimaces.

"We've been over for years now. I thought I made that clear when you got busted. I've moved on—you should do the same. Call Marla Jefferson for help. I haven't forgotten that you cheated on me twice with that skanky cougar—disgusting."

Elizabeth seems annoyed.

"I've got to go Adrian. Please don't call me again."

She shuts off her cell phone and sighs.

18
Boston

"That damn bitch is in for a rude awakening."

Adrian Dudley slams his cell phone down on a table in a dingy-looking motel room. He seems about to explode as he clenches his fist before pounding it on the table in a rage.

"That miserable slut needs to know who she's dealing with. I'm gonna fuck that bitch up so badly when I get to that stupid town where she lives. I'll make her beg for mercy."

He begins laughing loudly as he angrily throws the cell phone toward the mirror. It breaks into thousands of pieces.

TO BE CONTINUED

A Brief Look at the Fourth Episode

Relationship problems plague several people but for all the wrong reasons while a stranger plots to get his hands on something that doesn't belong to him as rivals seek to destroy each other.

Episode 4
Truth and Consequences

1

Gable Markway shakes hands with Eddie Kane and follows him into Eddie's office. He shuts the door and sighs loudly.

"Thanks for coming by on such short notice."

Gable nods as he faces Eddie again.

"You mentioned something about Bermuda?"

He seems uneasy.

"Said someone was attempting to stake a claim in what's left of the money that old man Madison left to Gina Bentley?"

Eddie wipes sweat from his brow.

"His name is Alec Martel."

Gable shakes his head. He watches as Eddie seems uneasy while he runs his fingers through his hair and sighs loudly.

"When we talked earlier you said something about him possibly being your half-brother? I'm assuming there's more to it than that for you to want my expertise. Blackmail scheme?"

Eddie grimaces as he sits down.

"Maybe—I can't get a read on him. He's probably about the same age as Gina—maybe a bit older but not much."

Page **95**

Gable reacts. Eddie notices and sighs loudly again.

"There's nothing on Martel to find anywhere on social media. No business contacts either—plenty of questions."

Eddie wrings his hands nervously.

"Warning signs everywhere about this Martel guy—I get the feeling there's a lot more than he's told us. I could use your help when it comes to figuring him out—see through him."

Gable seems confused.

"What about Pierce Colby?"

Eddie leans forward.

"This field of law isn't Colby's specialty. He recommended I get someone like you. I'm at a loss here when it comes to these turn of events involving yet another claim to overhaul what was already decided for several years now. I spoke with Carmen Pendleton earlier. She agrees with me about Martel as well—she thinks this guy might be after a big wad of cash from Gina."

Gable shoots Eddie a curious look.

"We don't know that yet—better to wait until he makes his move—tells us outright what he wants—but if he plays."

Eddie stands up.

"There's just something seriously shady about this whole situation—something reeks—why not earlier? Why now?"

Gable turns to face Eddie.

"Maybe he just found out he has Madison blood running through his veins—it's not totally out of the ordinary. Old man Madison played plenty of games with people's lives. My own daughter got caught up in your family's drama with that Sawyer boy—figured it out right away and gave some peace to Rachel McKinley—poor woman was haunted for years by the supposed death of her son—only to find out by accident that he was alive and well—that he had been given to one of Madison's employees to raise as their own. Played out as if it was one of those "ripped from the headlines" stories that NBC loved to dramatize."

Eddie gestures with his hand.

"How is Donna doing in Los Angeles?"

Gable runs his fingers through his hair and smiles.

"She works at CBS. Loves dealing with all those famous people she sees every day—much thanks to Alden Washington for getting her that job after she graduated from UCLA. The film business is tough to break into. He came through for her."

Eddie stifles a grin and wags his finger.

"Alden is a gem. Nice guy all around. He told me recently that Wesley is finally settling down after chasing women nonstop for years while he was in college. Made a baby with one of his girlfriends and took to fatherhood right away. That kid turned out much differently than we all thought. None of us ever imagined he'd make it through college much less graduate with a degree in movie making. Washington said Wesley is busy putting together a crew to begin filming his first movie on Catalina Island."

Gable points his finger at Eddie.

"Weren't you the one that said Wesley Madison would end up in jail for killing someone—said he was a frigging loser."

Eddie smirks and waves his hand in the air.

"Guilty—guilty as charged—but in my defense he seemed headed that way until Alden Washington came back to Marble Hills and triggered events that changed Wesley's life forever."

Gable gestures with his hand knowingly.

"Ashton hangs out with Wesley all the time when he's in Los Angeles. Who knew they'd have so much in common?"

Eddie walks over to where Gable is sitting and smirks.

"I bet you miss them something fierce?"

Gable gives Eddie a knowing look.

"Not a day goes by that I don't think about them. But they have their own lives to live. You have to let go at some point."

Eddie grimaces at the comment.

"I don't even want to think about Katrina and Laurel not needing me anymore. Being a father has been a highlight in my life after the terrible way I started out—best deal ever."

Gable stands and looks at his watch.

"Before we both start crying I think it's time I follow up on the Martel case and get back to you by tomorrow. I'm assuming you've told Gina Bentley about what has been playing out?"

Eddie watches Gable as he walks to the door.

"Pierce told her earlier—said she was handling it quite well given the circumstances. That girl has had more drama in her life than **Grace Metalious** could ever have dreamed of writing."

Gable nods in agreement.

"Except you, of course, old buddy—from troubled orphan to billionaire—quite the success story—perfect for a movie of the week—bet they could get **Milo Ventimiglia** to play you."

Eddie playfully shoves Gable.

"Hey, I can still belt you like I did when we were kids."

Gable grins broadly.

"Uh-huh—so you say anyway."

They pretend to shadowbox for a few seconds as they hug and Gable leaves. Eddie turns to look at the office and grins as he walks over to his desk. He grabs his cell phone and sighs.

"I think it's time I call Alden for a chat."

He begins dialing and smiles.

2

"Not interested in anything you have to offer."

Diane Gold glares at Malcolm Kemp as she sees his reaction to her slight. She points to the door several feet away.

"Get lost dweeb—be gone."

Malcolm sits down directly across from Diane. She seems annoyed and sighs loudly. He seems upset. She notices.

"I thought I made myself clear."

Diane looks at her cell phone lying nearby.

"Should I call Deputy Millner?"

Malcolm rolls his eyes.

"I'm not trying to score. I need your help."

Diane glances at Malcolm curiously.

"Is that so?"

Malcolm nods.

"I found out something about Robert Campo earlier."

Diane seems irritated and sighs loudly.

"Uh-huh—tell Robert he'll never get me in the backseat of his car. I'll never spread for that miserable creep—loser."

Malcolm seems nervous and shrugs.

"Robert is gay."

Diane suddenly seems interested and leans forward. She smiles at Malcolm. He drops his voice lower and whispers.

"He made a pass at me less than an hour ago."

Diane seems disgusted and shrugs.

"Robert likes women—slept with so many he can't even remember an exact number if his life depended on it."

Malcolm wipes sweat from his brow.

"I know—*I know*—he said it was all an act to keep from being outed—said he'd been playing both sides—thought he and I could get together—said he was tired of playing straight."

He leans back in the chair.

"I told him it wasn't my scene and he got upset. Called me all sorts of names—said I was a tease—swore he'd pop me."

Diane glances at her cell phone again.

"Ugh—wait until I tell Ashley."

Malcolm reacts and stands up.

"You can't tell Ashley—or anyone else."

Diane suddenly grabs her cell phone as Malcolm takes a step forward. He reaches out and grabs Diane by the arm.

"You can't—Robert will kill me."

Diane rolls her eyes.

"Watch me."

She begins dialing.

"That disgusting creep deserves to be outed after how he used Ashley and every other girl in this town. Ugh—pretending to be straight just to preserve his lousy reputation—gross."

Malcolm watches as Diane dials. He grins slyly as she looks away. She doesn't notice Robert Campo standing several yards away hidden by a few large potted shrubs. Malcolm sighs as Diane waits patiently for the line to be picked up. She looks at him briefly and shuts off the cell phone. She gestures at him.

"She must be at the movies or something."

Page **99**

Malcolm seems relieved and watches as Diane relaxes a little. He glances at Robert and signals him. He turns to face Diane again and sits down. She gives him a cautious look.

"I'm gonna crush Robert Campo. When I'm done with him he won't be able to show his face in Marble Hills again."

Malcolm reacts as Diane smiles broadly.

"Just forget what I said earlier, OK?"

Diane snaps her fingers.

"Not a chance—I intend to crucify that worm and bring him to his knees. He'll beg for mercy—I guarantee it."

At that moment Robert grabs Malcolm and shoves him to the ground as Diane reacts in shock. Robert kicks Malcolm several times as he pretends to be enraged. He seems disgusted.

"I warned you about telling anyone about what I told you earlier—especially with this frigging witch. I ought to break your fucking neck for stabbing me in the back right after I told you to keep a lid on it—some friend you are—you're a dead man."

Diane stands up and looks at her cell phone.

"You better leave before you get arrested for assault. One call is all it'll take—you have no fans at the police station."

Robert turns to look at Diane.

"Shut up bitch."

He kicks Malcolm again.

"You'll regret fucking me with me. You and me have unfinished business—prepare a funeral with a closed casket."

Robert glares at Diane for a second or two and then storms off. Diane turns to look at Malcolm. She comes toward him and offers him help to stand. He wipes away blood from his hand and faces Diane once more. She seems distressed at having witnessed what just happened. He notices and tries to smile.

"He's just playing around—I'll be OK."

She glances at the elevator a few yards away.

"I'll take you home. It's the least I can do."

She looks at him curiously and sighs.

"I'll have your car picked up later."

Malcolm nods and is led toward the elevator.

Page 100

3

Lyle Lincoln slowly puts his credit card back into his wallet as Melissa Marshall comes toward him. She grins broadly.

"Hello stranger."

Lyle turns around and sighs as he sees Melissa.

"I've been busy."

Melissa gives him a knowing look.

"What's her name?"

Lyle shrugs.

"You don't know her. She's from Pinecrest."

Melissa slides her arm around Lyle's waist and tugs at the buttons on his Levi's. He pulls away suddenly. She notices.

"What's going on? You and me go way back? Seen plenty of action between the sheets—played all sorts of games."

Lyle grins and seems nervous.

"I'm aware of our history—no need to go there."

Melissa reaches out to touch Lyle's jeans again. He pushes her hand away. He looks at her curiously and sighs loudly.

"We've been over for almost a month now."

Melissa winks at Lyle.

"You broke up with me—said you didn't like being one of my guys—wanted something more than casual flings."

Lyle nods and looks away.

"I've got things to do."

Melissa watches as he walks away.

"Damn him—he's nothing to me anyway. I can get any guy I want—he's used goods—played—nothing left to get."

She clenches her fist.

"I wonder who he found to occupy his time. Bet she's a cheap trollop—probably has a string of men she's discarded."

Melissa turns to look at Lyle as he gets into his car. She seems visibly upset. She clenches her fist again and sighs.

"I don't appreciate being slighted by one of my exes. I may have to teach him an ugly lesson—make him see the light."

She smiles broadly and licks her lips.

"Uh-huh—it's just a matter of time before I find out who he's been seeing and then I'll break them up. Oh—such joy."

She spins around several times.

Three Days Later

4

"We've got to stop meeting like this."

Steve Pendleton grins as he watches Alice Banning slide her finger across his exposed penis. She slyly glances at him as she continues to let her fingers play across the stiff expanse of his erection while he continues grinning. He laughs as she gives him a knowing look and aggressively pulls him forward. They kiss.

"You've got to ditch that ball and chain—you deserve better than that shrew dictating every move you make."

Steve wags his finger at Alice.

"We've had this conversation already—things are the way they are until I can figure things out between Ava and me. There's nothing left to discuss—I'm a married man—case closed."

Alice leans forward and tousles Steve's hair.

"A married man who's been sexually active with half of New England—you and I go way back—been through a lot."

Steve nods in agreement.

"I'm aware of our sexual history."

Alice jabs Steve.

"What about you and Marla Jefferson?"

Steve shrugs.

"What about her?"

Alice jabs Steve again.

"I've heard stories about her and some of her pool guys. She's playing around with teenage boys too—high school."

Steve laughs loudly and licks his lips.

"Someone has to teach them about how to satisfy a woman before they head off to college—kudos to her."

Page **102**

Alice pulls away from Steve. She seems irritated.

"I gather you have no problem with how promiscuous she's been—spreading her legs for every guy in town. Ugh—the nerve of someone like her to think she can get away with playing one man against the other. She's probably got an STD."

Steve makes a lewd gesture with his finger.

"You of all people shouldn't throw stones when it comes to being promiscuous. You have plenty history with guys all over this quaint town. You and Marla are cut from the same cloth."

Alice points her finger at Steve.

"I'm nothing like that man-stealing bitch."

Steve begins laughing.

"Keep telling yourself that."

He glances at the door and smirks.

"I guess I better get going."

Alice watches as he grabs his Levi's and begins dressing. She licks her lips several times as she watches him. He notices and strokes his penis several times. She blows him a kiss.

"I'm not done with this Marla situation."

Steve rolls his eyes.

"Marla is my business not yours."

Alice climbs out of bed.

"You can't have us both. Dangle us like tokens."

Steve winks at Alice and begins laughing.

"Uh-huh—like I said before—I'm done with this discussion concerning Marla. She and I are good friends—nothing more."

He smirks as he heads to the door.

"Say hi to Matt McFee for me."

Alice seems upset as she watches him leave.

"Seems to me Marla Jefferson needs a scandal to really wreck havoc in her life—I think it's time I pay a visit to Adam."

She grabs her cell phone.

"I wonder if Adam Westerfeldt still likes blowjobs as much as he did when he was my mother's charming pool boy."

Alice begins dialing furiously and then stops suddenly.

"Mother said he really knew how to please women."

Alice licks her lips several times and smiles.

"Forbid me from bedding him. Said he was hers and no one else's—of course that was before she caught him bedding Caroline Bentley—my mother kicked Adam to the curb right after and made sure everyone knew his deal. Not a pretty picture."

She looks at her cell phone again and smiles.

"I heard he lives in Bar Harbor now."

Alice begins dialing again and sighs loudly as she waits for a few seconds before the line is picked up. She grins broadly.

"Hello—I'm not sure if you remember me."

She nods several times and laughs.

5
Castle Beach

"The story about the Nix estate is old news."

Jessica Sago leans back in her chair as she looks at Greg Petrie for a few seconds. She seems confused and shrugs.

"It's just a bunch of fabricated tall tales."

Greg gives Jessica a sharp look.

"Eddie Kane just purchased the old Nix estate. Said he's gonna clean it up and turn the property into a park."

Jessica reacts and sighs loudly.

"My brother died on that property if you recall—place is creepy. There's an old cemetery and mausoleum there too. Like who'd want to go there—especially late at night—ugh."

Greg stands up.

"I know what happened to your brother and several of his friends on the estate. There was never a really good explanation if you recall from either Parker Ross or David Sherwood."

Jessica seems uneasy.

"My brother's body was never found."

Greg walks over to where Jessica is sitting.

"Precisely—it never made sense to me that the CDC was never able to locate your brother's remains. Too many answers left without a reliable explanation. Quite odd if you ask me."

Page **104**

Jessica looks at Greg curiously.

"Are you saying what I think you're saying?"

Greg runs his fingers through his hair.

"Where are those boys anyway? Last I heard they were living somewhere on the West Coast—California maybe?"

Jessica shakes her head.

"David and Parker are living in Los Angeles at the moment. Justine told me they lived for a while in San Francisco too. David also lived in a little town called Ocean Landing from what she said—Parker got a job at Paramount Pictures. David has been trying to sell his first screenplay—having a tough go at it."

Greg points his finger at Jessica.

"Where's Justine Ross at the moment?"

Jessica looks at Greg curiously.

"Why?"

Greg sighs.

"I think she knows plenty."

Jessica glances at her cell phone.

"She lives in Boston. Works for a lawyer named Jeremy Winterfield. I think I may still have her phone number."

Greg clasps his hands together.

"Call her—see what falls out of the tree."

Jessica nods in agreement.

"What about that story you had me follow up in Marble Hills—plenty there to focus on concerning what I found out."

Greg glances at the door.

"I see no reason you can't do both at the same time."

Jessica gives Greg a knowing look.

6

Lyle grins broadly as Katrina Kane pushes him backwards. He stumbles several times before falling onto the sand at Bradford Beach. Katrina points her finger at him and sighs.

"You bailed on me the other day."

Lyle begins laughing.

Page 105

"I forgot—had a lot of things to do."

Katrina sits down next to him.

"Uh-huh—I'll just bet you did. Disrespecting your girlfriend is a serious mistake—oh yeah—I could take it personally."

Lyle and Katrina stand up.

"I just don't want to do something that you might regret later. Giving yourself to me is a major move on your part."

Katrina slides her arms around Lyle's waist.

"I want you to take my virginity as you promised me you would on our first date—said you wouldn't take no for an answer if I recall. Said I would be your girl—said it was a done deal."

"Me and my big frigging mouth—I should've quit while I still could—told you I had issues—was bad in bed—terrible."

Katrina strokes Lyle's cheek.

"You've been wonderful—but enough is enough—I want you to be my first—to add me to your long list of conquests."

Lyle gestures with his hand.

"What if after we sleep together you begin wishing it hadn't happened—it'll be too late—once I'm inside you there's no turning back—you'll have lost your virginity forever."

Katrina hugs Lyle warmly.

"That's exactly why I want you to be my first. You're such a nice guy—so caring and sensitive—always thinking."

Lyle kisses Katrina once more.

"What about your father—he'll end my life if he gets wind of what you and I are talking about—broke my neck."

Katrina rolls her eyes.

"My father is harmless—he's all talk. I know him better than you—besides I've got him wrapped him around my little finger so tight he can't breathe—nothing to be afraid about."

Lyle makes a slashing motion with his finger across his neck as Katrina seems annoyed at his behavior. He sighs.

"If I end up dead it'll be your fault."

Katrina lets her fingers slide across Lyle's belt. He grins as she begins to tug at the buckle. She pulls it loose and smirks.

"You've got nowhere to run—I expect results."

She begins unbuttoning the buttons on his Levi's as his erection begins to show. He watches her fingers as her hand slips inside his underwear. He lets out a moan as she touches him.

"You don't play fair—a guy can only resist the wicked machinations of his virginal girlfriend. I'm in serious trouble."

Katrina watches his reaction as she strokes his penis for several seconds. He looks at the blanket nearby and grins.

"This will be your doing—I'm at your mercy."

Katrina pushes Lyle down on the blanket and sighs.

"I've never felt this way about anyone."

She unbuttons his Levi's further.

"I won't regret one moment of being with you."

Lyle kisses Katrina lightly then more passionately as they slowly lie backwards on the blanket and continues kissing. They kiss several more times as he begins pulling at her blouse and laughs. Katrina strokes Lyle's cheek again and pledges her love for him once more as they begin making love for the first time.

7

"Why are you telling me this now? It's been years since William Crenshaw died. It was ruled an accident. He fell off a pier in Marble Hills—according to the press he was showing off to Gina Bentley while walking on one of the guardrails and fell onto the rocks below. There was no story—just a dead end."

Nola French glances at the manuscript in her hands.

"What are you planning to do with this?"

Lynne Crenshaw grins slyly.

"Publish it of course—I've got an agent already. The truth has to come out one way or the other—people need to know what really happened—Gina Bentley murdered my cousin."

Nola gestures with her hand.

"She'll sue you the minute the book comes out. That girl has tons of cash—she'll ruin you. I'd think twice about going through with your plans if I were you Lynne. She has a lot of powerful people around her too—Eddie Kane is her brother."

Lynne waves her hand in the air and smiles broadly.

"I'm not worried about Eddie Kane or anyone else for that matter. Gina Bentley murdered my cousin and she has to pay."

Nola looks at the manuscript again.

"Don't say I didn't warn you."

Lynne grabs the manuscript and flips through it.

"She's a killer—she killed a whole bunch of people not long after William turned up dead—she should be in jail."

Nola seems annoyed and sighs loudly.

"Gina Bentley didn't kill anyone. It was her deranged sister that did the killings. She was certifiable from what I heard."

Lynne waves the manuscript in Nola's face.

"That Parker girl took the blame after the fact. It was Gina that killed everyone and got away with it—including killing my cousin. Justice must be served—even for rich people."

Nola shakes her head several times.

8

"I'm glad we've gotten to know each other better."

Diane looks at Malcolm as they walk along the sidewalk outside Springview Mall. He reaches out to take her hand.

"I had a good time earlier. The movie sucked chunks but the company was wonderful. I'd like to do it again."

Diane smiles as she looks at Malcolm.

"I had a good time also. You were the perfect gentlemen. Nothing like what I imagined—quite charming too."

Malcolm grins broadly.

"How about we head to Mayflower Beach? The place is always deserted. Not much people around this time of year."

Diane looks at Malcolm with a knowing look. He notices.

"We could walk along the surf and talk. Nothing more I promise—just talk. Might be fun actually—find out stuff about each other that we didn't know about—learn new things."

Diane nods several times and seems pleased.

"Hopefully Robert won't show up."

Page **108**

Malcolm grimaces and shakes his head.

"He's probably banging some homo dude in town as we speak—or maybe that guy he said he knows from Portland."

Diane shoots Malcolm a curious look.

"What guy in Portland?"

Malcolm runs his fingers through his hair.

9
Bermuda

"Uh-huh—good—she's taken the bait—it's just a matter of time before she springs that juicy story on Gina Bentley. Makes her life even more complicated than before—create chaos."

Alec Martel grins broadly as he walks back and forth on the old-fashioned wrought iron balcony overlooking the ocean as he talks on his cell phone. He stops suddenly and laughs.

"Of course I know what I'm doing. Keep planting seeds and I assure you Gina Bentley will be brought to justice."

He gestures with his hand.

"I'm headed your way within a few hours—laying the groundwork before I make my presence known to my stupid relatives. They have no idea what I have in store for them."

He begins laughing.

"Exactly—things will never be the same again after I get through with my clueless half-sister. She'll learn exactly how the game is played when I'm done with her. I intend to turn her life into a frigging nightmare—turn her into a mental case ready for a padded room in some swanky nuthouse outside of Boston."

Alec slowly turns to face the ocean again.

"Keep up plying that busybody with information about Gina Bentley—it's just a matter of days before she starts blabbing to her friends and from there it'll spread like wildfire. Nothing they'll do will make a difference after people begin to talk."

He stops suddenly and seems annoyed.

"Of course not Lynne—do I look like a fool?"

He clenches his fist several times and sighs loudly.

"Just do what I said and leave the thinking to me."

He clenches his fist again.

"That's right—I know how to play the game—had plenty of experience screwing people all across this island. When I get to Marble Hills there will be no stopping my plans. That damn bitch had no right to sink all that money into a frigging school. I want my share of my father's money and nothing and no one will stand in my way—least of all some half-crazy girl with no future."

He nods a few more times.

10

Denver Skiffington lies back on the blanket inside his van and grins broadly as he faces Mariska Benson. He smirks.

"Oh yeah, nothing like good sexual play to relax a guy like me after he's had a tough morning—quite the sweet deal."

Mariska leans closer to Denver.

"You're lucky I'm even speaking to you after how you've been treating me—I thought I made my point clear about Eden Penney. She's off limits—you don't need her—she's a slut."

Denver points his finger at Mariska.

"I don't recall agreeing to being ordered around by one of my girls. I'm a single guy. I can fuck whom I want whenever I find the opportunity. You and I are just friends—with benefits."

Mariska seems irritated.

"I don't see what you see in her anyway."

Denver laughs.

"She spreads her legs for me."

He makes a lewd gesture with his finger and laughs.

"Do I have to say more?"

Mariska jabs Denver and sits up. She turns back to face him with a malicious glint in her eye. She licks her lips.

"It would be too bad if someone accidentally dropped hints that Eden and her brother were more than just brother and sister. Imagine the talk that could result—oh, the scandal."

Denver shoots Mariska a dirty look.

Page 110

"Don't you go round town spreading lies about Eden Penney—her family has powerful lawyers—they'll ruin you."

Mariska begins laughing.

"That girl has no money—after her father kicked the bucket her money evaporated. She's as poor as the rest of us in Marble Hills. I'm not worried about her coming after me."

She gestures with her hand.

"I can handle her—but the question is—will you still continue sleeping with that cheap slut if people begin talking."

Denver sits up and grabs Mariska's arm.

"Uh-huh—you betcha—I'm still gonna stick her no matter what you do—give it up Mariska. I'm not your property."

Mariska pulls away from Denver.

"I hate you."

Denver snickers.

"Do I look like I care?"

Mariska glares at Denver for a few seconds and begins pulling on her blouse. He leans back on the blanket and grins.

11

Ashley Brewster sips on a mug of iced coffee as Timothy Bradley walks over to her and sits down. She faces him.

"Get lost—just leave me alone."

Timothy reacts and sighs loudly. He stands.

"We're not all bad—some of us are actually nice."

Ashley rolls her eyes.

"Uh-huh—tell that to the girls you cheated on and then pretended it was no big deal. You're no better than Robert."

Timothy slowly runs his fingers through his hair.

"Robert Campo and I are nothing alike."

He watches as Ashley takes another sip and shrugs.

"Keep telling yourself that and maybe one day it'll actually become reality—in the meantime it's not—bye Timmy."

He gives her a curious look and walks away.

"I bet he's gonna call Robert."

She takes another sip of the iced coffee and notices Lacey Arlington looking at her curiously. Lacey comes over seconds later and sits next to Ashley. They look at each other.

"I heard about Robert."

Ashley winces.

"He was all wrong for me."

Lacey nods.

"Human males are a strange breed. They just can't see what's in front of them—have to be led all the time or they lose focus and end up lost and bewildered. No hope out there that they'll somehow evolve over time—been that way forever."

Ashley shrugs and faces Lacey.

"He cheated on me and lied about it."

Lacey reaches out to pat Ashley on the shoulder.

"Been there plenty of times with my exes. They can't keep it in their pants long enough to understand how much damage they do when they move from bed to bed with the latest flavor of the week—who just happens to be a skanky whore."

Ashley laughs.

"Sounds just like Robert."

She takes another sip of the iced coffee.

"I just want to meet someone who likes me for me and not because I'm another mark to be played and checked. I get so mad when I think of how he used me and didn't care that he did."

Lacey leans closer to Ashley.

"My daughter had plenty of issues worrying with cheating boyfriends when she was your age. But it all worked out in the end—she found a nice guy and married him. They have two kids now. It just takes a while to wade through all the toads."

Ashley winces again.

"Uh-huh—that's exactly what Robert is—a toad."

She gestures with her hand.

"I wish he was dead."

Lacey appears alarmed at the comment and leans over to hug Ashley. Ashley seems upset as tears come to her eyes.

Page 112

"How are you feeling today?"

Charlene McColl turns around to face her husband as he grins slyly. She sighs loudly as Will McColl comes toward her with open arms. They hug warmly for a few seconds. He laughs.

"This dad business is serious for an expectant father. I can't stop thinking about delivery day. Scared a bit too if you must know—never had to be responsible for another person before. It's a whole new deal—lots of things to worry about."

Charlene tousles Will's hair.

"You'll do fine—you've got nothing to worry about. I know you're going to make a wonderful father—Maxwell says so by the way. He thinks I got lucky when it came to marrying you."

Will hugs Charlene warmly again.

"When is your wayward brother going to show his face in Marble Hills again—seems to me he should be making a nuisance of himself now that's he's about to become an uncle. Especially with all the work he put into making sure you got me to the altar just three months after we met—left nothing to chance."

Charlene pretends to slap Will.

"My brother didn't do anything special where you're concerned—I did it all—I chased you for weeks after the first time we met—made sure you didn't slip through my fingers."

Will laughs and wags his finger at Charlene.

"So, you actually admit it—you chased after me."

Charlene jabs Will in the chest.

"There's nothing wrong with a woman seeing something she wants and going after it—I wanted you—I admit it."

Will grins broadly and hugs Charlene.

"It was nice to be wanted after the terrible dry spell I had before we met—didn't have to do anything special."

Charlene wipes a tear from her eye. Will notices as she tries to regain her composure. He pulls her toward him. They look at each other for a few seconds. Will kisses her lightly.

"Did I say something wrong?"

Charlene shakes her head and hugs Will. She wipes away another tear and hugs him again. She seems about to cry.

"I got exactly what I always wanted. A wonderful man to spend the rest of my life with—you're just so sweet—kind."

"I'm yours for as long as you want me—got nowhere else to go—no one else will ever spoil me as badly as you have."

She gives him a knowing look.

"Are you admitting you have it too good?"

He begins laughing and nods.

"I'm so badly spoiled—my life is too easy—got a wife that adores me—got a brother-in-law that thinks I'm right for his demanding sister—and now I'm about to become a father."

He points his finger at her.

"Only thing missing is a large pile of cash."

Charlene seems about to laugh as she hugs Will again.

13

Bar Harbor

"I don't know what else I can say—she and I are over—we cut ties when I started dating my wife. Marla didn't take to kindly to me making a play for her best friend's virginal daughter."

Adam Westerfeldt watches Alice's reaction as she shoots him a cautious look and takes a step forward. He sighs.

"She said I was a louse for trying to score with a virgin."

He runs his fingers through his hair.

"Maya got pregnant the first time we had sex."

He watches her reaction.

"I had to marry her—she was pregnant and wouldn't get an abortion—I was in a bad way at that moment. Her brother made threats against my life—left no doubt he'd kill me."

Alice reaches out to stroke Adam's chest.

"Oh how horrible for you to be threatened by some guy you hardly knew—he sounds like a brute—cold-blooded."

Adam gives Alice a knowing look.

"He and I have actually become good friends."

Page 114

He glances at the ocean.

"What exactly do you want from me?"

Alice pulls Adam toward her. She grins slyly.

"I want to take Marla Jefferson down."

She makes a slashing motion with her finger across her neck several times. He takes a step back and shakes his head.

"I've got nothing for you. She and I are not on speaking terms—don't know what game she's playing now. Sorry."

Alice glances at his Levi's and sighs.

"Don't tell me you've been faithful since you tied the knot with that cow. Ugh—a guy being faithful is dull and boring."

Adam runs his fingers through his hair again.

"My wife is not a cow."

Alice seems upset and faces the ocean briefly. She faces him again and aggressively tugs at his belt buckle. He winces.

"Nothing is gonna happen with us—I took vows. I intend to keep them—I'm not the guy I used to be. Fatherhood made me see life in a whole different way—got to live life right."

Alice seems appalled at his behavior.

"Ugh—I've never been so viciously insulted by someone so good-looking and charming. What is this world coming to when hot guys are faithful to their boring wives—*ugh*—I'm so gone."

He watches her storm off and sighs loudly.

14

"Tough break buddy—got slighted by Ashley on the first try—glad I'm not you—that sting is gonna hurt for a while."

Kelvin Penney looks at Timothy and laughs.

"Look on the bright side—the sex would've been terrible anyway. According to Campo she was lousy in bed. Didn't give good blow either—he said she was stiff and unimaginative."

Timothy rolls his eyes.

"I wouldn't listen to a word Campo says. He's a spiteful liar. He thinks every girl should swoon whenever he's around."

He laughs and jabs Kelvin several times.

"It's no skin off my nose—I've got a whole slew of girls to pick from if I choose to—starting with the Benson sisters."

Kelvin makes a lewd gesture with his finger.

"They don't do nerds. They like buff guys—dumb jocks that talk in monosyllables—and flex their arms constantly."

Timothy gives Kelvin a knowing look.

"I assume you got shot down plenty of times by the Benson sisters—probably begged plenty too—troubling."

Kelvin grimaces and jabs Timothy again.

"I'm long over the Benson sisters—too many other girls that are willing to spread—no need to be tied to one chick."

He laughs and gestures with his hand.

"Besides, I've met someone new—unique."

Timothy leans against the railing of the pier and looks out at the ocean. He turns to face Kelvin again and grins.

"How much does she charge?"

Kelvin shakes his fist at Timothy.

"I'm gonna let that one slide on account of how pathetic you seem right now. This girl is different. She's not the type to follow the usual herds—she has spunk. Saw her yesterday while I was visiting with my lawyer—she's definitely someone I'd like to get to know better. She's pretty and knows who she is—not like some of the other girls I've been with lately—seriously classy."

Timothy sticks his finger into his mouth.

"Does this wonder have a name? Do I know her?"

Kelvin shakes his head.

"Doubt it—she attends Pinecrest."

Timothy reacts.

"Ugh—yuk—she's another Marla Sherwood no doubt. A selfish stuck-up bitch and a know-it-all—you can have her."

Kelvin seems upset and shoves Timothy.

"She's nothing like Marla. She's sweet and doesn't mouth off about every political topic that comes into her mind."

Timothy sticks his finger into his mouth again and pretends to puke over the side of the railing. Kelvin sighs.

"Do you even know her name?"

Kelvin runs his fingers through his hair and shrugs.

"I'm still working on that."

Timothy begins laughing loudly.

15
Castle Beach

Jessica turns to face Greg as she shuts off her cell phone. She seems somewhat confused as she notices his stare.

"Well, what did Justine Ross say?"

Jessica gestures with her hand.

"Not much—she said her brother never talked about what happened in detail before he left for college. Said something about whatever happened to Preston and the others never made sense. She got the idea that whatever it was that turned his body into goo was never explained. Made a weird comment that Parker was still messed up over what occurred and stated he refused to come back to Castle Beach—said he was really happy in Los Angeles—didn't want to think about what happened."

Greg leans back in his chair and sighs.

"Seems to me there must be plenty left to talk about what happened in Castle Beach a while back. I think you should pay Justine a friendly visit tomorrow—spark a long-ago memory."

Jessica wags her finger at Greg.

"No way am I going to Boston to harass one of my friends for a nonexistent story. If there was any juice the CDC would have let everyone in Castle Beach know what they found. Even they had no answer for what they dealt with. Whatever happened went away as soon as it started—probably some bug that Chris Gibson came across at the Nix estate and spread around town."

Greg stands up and walks over to Jessica.

"Uh-huh—exactly why this story is so relevant at this moment. Eddie Kane is planning to renovate the old Nix estate shortly. We certainly don't want whatever afflicted Chris Gibson to rear its ugly head again. Forget talking to Justine Ross at the moment—what about Gibson's relatives? What's their deal?"

Jessica shakes her head and glances at her cell phone.

"I really don't know the family other than Chris and Parker were cousins—and that Chris was sort of a hothead."

Greg takes a step forward.

"I'll expect results soon."

Jessica nods and turns away.

16

Marla Jefferson slams her cell phone down on a table and seems ready to explode. She turns to face Dina Brown.

"That damn bitch has nerve to talk trash about me—that woman slept with her husband's brother—and got pregnant."

Dina reacts and glances at the other patrons inside the diner as people begin looking at Marla. She gestures nervously.

"Alice was married?"

Marla nods several times.

"It lasted about a year. Husband was away in New York but he came home early and found his trashy wife in bed with his sleazy brother. Marriage was kaput soon after. The baby shocker came immediately after. Her ex's brother refused to marry her so she aborted the child—tried to say later that she miscarried."

Marla gives Dina a knowing look.

"Everyone knew the truth regardless. That woman is a piece of work—has a really bad reputation—and now she's talking trash about me behind my back. From what my friend in Bar Harbor said Alice was seen trying to cozy up with one of my exes in order to get dirt on me. But she failed—apparently she struck out with Adam. He wouldn't put out—pissed her off royally."

She makes a lewd gesture with her finger.

"This is war nevertheless—I'll crucify that bitch."

She leans toward Dina.

"I know things about her."

She watches Dina's reactions and grins.

"The next couple of days will be highly unpleasant for Alice—no one crosses me and gets away with it—no one."

Dina watches as Marla grabs her cell phone.

"What are you going to do?"

Marla licks her lips and begins dialing furiously.

"That whore has been keeping a secret and I think it's time everyone in Marble Hills knew exactly what I know."

Marla's demeanor changes suddenly.

"It happened right before Alice moved to town and began sleeping with every virile man dumb enough to drop his pants for her. Uh-huh—that slut's not gonna like this game one bit."

Marla grins broadly as the line is picked up.

"Hello Carlos."

She licks her lips again.

"Uh-huh—I know—it's been a while."

She leans back in the chair and seems really pleased.

"How would you like to pay me a visit?"

She nods several times and glances at Dina.

17

Alice sighs loudly as she watches Matt McFee leaving the gym. As he begins walking across the parking lot she steps out of her car. He stops as he sees her. He seems nervous and sighs.

"I get the impression you've been avoiding me lately."

Matt waves his hand in the air.

"Laura is on the warpath again—you and I have to chill for a while—play it cool until she loses interest. No contact."

Alice suddenly grabs Matt by the arm.

TO BE CONTINUED

A Brief Look at the Fifth Episode

Several schemes are set in motion to destroy hated rivals as an unexpected visitor plays games with the truth while secrets from the past comes back to cause grief for one specific person.

Episode 5

Once Upon a Time

1

"I didn't realize I was going that fast."

Adrian Dudley looks at the deputy officer and seems annoyed at being bothered at all. Scott Millner gives Adrian a knowing look and sighs loudly. He looks at the pad in his hand.

"Don't let me catch you speeding again. Marble Hills isn't Portland—we don't like having traffic mishaps here."

Adrian rolls his eyes.

"I understand."

He watches as Scott walks toward his patrol car just a few yards away. He makes a lewd gesture with his hand.

"Loser—that dude probably thinks his pathetic job makes him cool or something—like give me a fucking break."

He snickers and looks at Scott again.

"That guy better stay out of my way or he'll get what's coming to him—right after I teach Elizabeth Pendleton a lesson for ratting me out to the cops and sending me to prison."

He clenches his fist several times.

"Uh-huh—she and I have plenty to talk about."

He slams his fist against the steering wheel and grimaces.

"Heard she got herself a new guy right after I got sent up the river—threw me over like I didn't matter. I swear I'll kill her with my bare hands for the shame she brought me—take her out like trash and that boyfriend of hers too—end him royally."

He laughs and pulls out a small handgun.

2

Taylor Pendleton sighs as he looks at the handful of bills in his hand. He seems upset as Lacey Arlington comes toward him with another mug of coffee. He faces her and grimaces.

"Bills are piling up—never knew being an adult was gonna be so worrisome—college degree seems useless at the moment given how hard it is to find a job in this town—fuck."

Lacey gives Taylor a knowing look.

"I've got a friend down the coast that could use your skills at website design. He mentioned to me he needed his site to be updated in a jiffy—maybe you should check with him—I got his number if you want it? Couldn't hurt to give him a call?"

Taylor stifles a smile.

"Is he your ex?"

Lacey wags her finger at Taylor.

"Bite your tongue—he's just a friend and nothing more. Besides Greg Petrie is a happily married man with two kids."

Taylor rolls his eyes.

"Since when has that stopped anyone?"

Lacey wags her finger at Taylor again and sighs.

"Not everyone is your father."

She watches his reaction and looks around.

"The change of scenery might do you some good. Castle Beach is quite a ways away from Marble Hills. Just outside of Boston—less than ten miles from Plymouth. Good people."

Taylor wipes sweat from his brow.

"I know where it is—been there several times—dated a girl named Justine Ross while I was in college who lived there."

Lacey reaches out to pat Taylor on the shoulder.

"See, you've got a friend already."

Taylor waves his hand.

"Justine lives in Boston now."

Lacey reacts.

3

"I already told you we have to cool it."

Matt McFee runs his fingers through his hair.

"I've got a full plate right now."

Alice Banning pushes Matt against the door of the gym and kisses him. She seems irritated as he tries to pull away.

"You and I are good together. Laura is a zero—she needs to step aside and set you free. I'm tired of her rude attitude."

Matt sighs loudly and turns away.

"It's over for the time being."

Alice aggressively grabs at Mike's shorts.

"It's over when I decide. That bitch isn't going to dictate to me who I can and can't sleep with. You and I are good together in bed and that's all that matters. It's time to cut her loose."

Sounds of footsteps can be heard right behind them and as they turn they see Nola French looking disdainfully at them.

"Just can't keep your filthy husband-stealing hands off every man in this town—have you no shame—no respect."

Alice makes a lewd gesture with her finger.

"I'm really getting tired of you."

"Oh, I'll just bet."

Matt takes a step forward.

"It's not what it looks like Nola."

Nola glares at Matt and then faces Alice.

4

Father Vincent slowly walks across the front lawn of a quaint-looking church and glances at the open gate nearby.

"I'm sure I closed it earlier. The latch must have slipped."
He hears a laugh and faces Melissa Marshall.
"Hello Vincent—it's been a while."
He reacts and sighs.
"I'd prefer you call me Father Vincent."
Melissa rolls her eyes.
"I'm sure you would—and I would if I respected you—but since I know what I know about you—you're Vincent to me."
He recoils and takes a step forward.
"Perhaps you should leave."
Melissa makes a lewd gesture with her finger.
"I bet Marlene's tongue was magic—bet you enjoyed every minute—too bad I know what you two did together."
His expression changes suddenly.
"I don't know what you're talking about."
Melissa gives him a knowing look and begins laughing.
"Uh-huh—I wonder how the church board will feel about what I know—it'll be such a shame if they saw my video."
Father Vincent slowly takes another step toward Melissa.
"Marlene Benson and I are just friends."
"Last time I checked friends don't give blowjobs to men of the cloth—the question is how many have you received so far from that wretched tramp—how many has it been Vincent?"
She watches as he clenches his fist.
"I want you to leave right now."
Melissa looks at her cell phone and grins.
"Just one click Vincent and your world is gonna be blown sky high—think about that. You have one hour to decide."
"What exactly do you want?"
Melissa grins broadly.

5

"I've wondered about them for a while now. No brother and sister are that close—ugh—I think I'm gonna be sick."
Mariska Benson grins and faces Diane Gold.

Page **124**

"Imagine if they made a baby together?"

Diane seems upset and sighs.

"Have you been drinking?"

Mariska licks her lips.

"Ask Denver if you don't believe me."

Mariska wags her finger at Diane.

"Denver saw them kissing—making out at Mayflower Beach too—going at it like some freak show horror movie."

Mariska licks her lips several times.

"They were so hot for each other—it was like one of those movies where a redneck family lives in a trailer park—having sex with each other and making babies—straight up perverted."

Mariska pretends to be disgusted.

"That whole family is messed up. Kelvin's dad was a terrible human being from what I heard—cheated on his wife and caused her to die of a drug overdose—then he just up and died one night from what I heard. Kelvin and Eden ended up with nothing—had to come here to live with their housekeeper."

Diane seems bored.

"Didn't Kelvin's father die of a heart attack?"

Mariska nods and then whispers.

"That was what was reported—but I heard the real story was that he killed himself—the heart attack story was a sham."

Mariska gestures with her hand.

"No wonder Kelvin and Eden are so close—all that hugging led to touching and then they began doing each other when they thought no one was looking. Ugh—gross."

Diane grabs her cell phone.

6

"She did what? How dare she spew lies?"

Marlene Benson slams her fist against the steering wheel of her car as several cars drive by. She sighs loudly.

"I'll take care of it—she's gone too far this time."

She nods several times and seems about to explode.

Page **125**

"I'll check back with you shortly."

She shuts off her cell phone as she pulls over to the side of the road. She looks at herself in the rearview mirror.

"That bitch is gonna pay."

She begins dialing and seems pleased.

7

Boston

"I'll see you shortly. Uh-huh—just got a few things to take care of before I arrive in Marble Hills within the next hour."

Alec Martel gestures with his hand.

"No doubt—my dear half-sister has no idea what I have planned for her later this week. Heads will roll no doubt."

He begins laughing and seems annoyed.

"Of course I'm aware of what exactly is at stake."

He gestures again and sighs loudly.

8

Lynne Crenshaw shuts off her cell phone and glances at the manuscript lying on top of a coffee table a few feet away.

"I've waited so long for this day."

She wipes sweat from her brow and sighs.

"Poor William has waited so long for justice to be served after what happened to him—he had so much to live for."

She clenches her fist several times.

"But that evil girl took it all away when she pushed him off the railing at Stanley Pier. Pushed him off and lied about it."

She walks over to the coffee table.

"It's just a matter of time now before it all comes full circle and she gets what she has so richly deserved for years now."

She wipes a tear from her eye.

"Revenge will be so sweet—sweet indeed—I'll destroy her the way she destroyed poor William—payback is a bitch."

She slowly reaches for the manuscript.

Page **126**

9

Elizabeth Pendleton walks to the door as the doorbell rings again. She reaches for the doorknob. As she opens the door she sees Adrian standing in the doorway with a gun pointed at her. He suddenly bursts out laughing and gestures at her.

"Time's up, *bitch*—I told you you'd be seeing me soon enough. No one dumps me and gets away with it—time for you to pay for your sins—you and that clown boyfriend of yours."

He forces his way into the apartment as she slowly backs away. Elizabeth seems to be in shock as he takes a step forward and grins broadly while he waves the gun in his hand at her.

"Who do you think you were dumping me the way you did? You had no right to shove me aside like trash after what we meant to each other. You owe me—and I intend to collect."

Elizabeth glances at her cell phone on the kitchen counter several yards away. Adrian notices and begins laughing.

"You'll never make it—I swear I'll pop you right here and now—one bullet straight through your empty skull and your lights will go out forever. I've become a much different man because of prison—of which you sent me to—lied about me to the cops."

Elizabeth sighs loudly.

"I didn't lie. You were guilty."

Adrian becomes enraged and looks at his gun.

"I did nothing wrong. Those kids wanted to buy drugs. I was only giving them what they wanted—an innocent man went to prison because his bitch of a girlfriend squealed on him."

Elizabeth watches Adrian as he comes closer.

"I would never have had to serve time in that filthy hellhole if you had kept your mouth shut—you owe me."

He begins laughing loudly as he waves the gun in the air.

"I think it's only fair you lose your life at my hands because of what you did to me—no one would blame me for righting a wrong that was done to me by ending your miserable life."

Adrian takes another step and grimaces.

"If you leave now I won't say anything. I'll pretend this never happened. Pretend you never came by today. No one will ever know about your visit. I promise I won't say anything."

Adrian looks at Elizabeth curiously and begins laughing hysterically. He waves the gun around for several seconds.

"Do I look like a moron? You're not gonna tell anyone anything because you'll be dead, *bitch*—killed by my gun."

He looks around at the apartment.

"Where's that stupid boyfriend of yours?"

Elizabeth remains silent as Adrian looks at the gun in his hand again and then at the front door. He begins laughing.

"He's a dead man walking regardless."

He laughs even louder.

"One shot to the temple and he's done for—and then I'll take care of that frigging loser Eddie Kane. Hiring that lawyer to prosecute me was a mistake. That bastard is gonna pay dearly for slighting me—he'll beg for mercy—before I shoot him."

He suddenly lunges at Elizabeth.

10

Nola sits down at a corner table as Lacey comes over to her with a mug of coffee. Nola smiles as she sees Lacey.

"You look like someone who just got her hands on really important information on someone you don't like—hate—let me guess—Alice Banning just stole someone else's husband."

Nola rolls her eyes.

"Matt McFee."

Lacey reacts and sighs loudly.

"That man just keeps digging himself a deeper grave every time he dallies with that woman—you'd think he'd know better by now. He better hope that Laura doesn't find out."

Nola grins broadly.

"Matt has a nasty surprise waiting for him when he gets home. Laura is fit to be tied. She's probably packing his bags at this very moment—and planning to make Alice pay dearly."

Lacey gestures with her hand.

"Do you think that was such a good idea Nola? Matt will be furious you outed him—he'll come after you with guns blazing when he finds out. That man has a nasty temper—vicious."

Nola takes a sip from the mug.

"Matt doesn't scare me—one word from me and he'll end up in jail—stuck being roomies with some homeless druggie."

She snickers and begins laughing.

"He brought this situation on himself. Running all over town with that tramp—he should know better. Alice Banning has had plenty of romps with the men in this area. I doubt there's a man she hasn't made a play for—there's even rumors she bedded Father Vincent—not that it would be a stretch for him—word has it that he's been playing doctor with several of the women from his church. Makes that book *Thorn Birds* by **Colleen McCullough** seem tame by comparison—such horrid behavior—sick."

Lacey gives Nola a strange look.

11

Lyle Lincoln looks at Katrina Kane as he slowly folds up the blanket they were laying on moments before. He grins.

"I hope you're OK with what happened?"

Katrina reaches out to kiss Lyle.

"I'm perfectly OK with what happened between us. It was everything I imagined it to be. You were simply wonderful."

They look at each other. He sighs.

"I think for now we should keep what just happened between us private—no need to give anyone ammunition."

Katrina rolls her eyes.

"My father won't lay a finger on you."

Lyle shakes his head.

"Uh-huh—so you say—but when he finds out I did his little girl he'll have my head on a platter. I'll be dead by nightfall."

Katrina slides her hands around Lyle's waist.

"I won't let my father hurt you."

Page **129**

Lyle pulls away and heads toward the entrance of the beach where his car is parked. He stops and grins slyly.

"How are you with threesomes?"

Katrina makes a slashing gesture with her finger.

12

Laura McFee glances at the images on her cell phone and seems about to explode as her rage grows. She clenches her fist several times before turning to face an oil painting on a wall a few feet away. She sighs loudly and slowly walks over to it.

"That bitch is done for—no more chances."

She quickly moves the painting aside and begins turning the tumbler on a combination lock. Laura smiles broadly.

"She won't see it coming—one blast—just one."

She grins as she pulls out a small handgun. As she closes the door to the safe she hears the front door opening. She spins around to see Matt standing in the doorway. As he closes the door he realizes Laura is holding a gun. He seems in shock.

"What are you doing with that?"

Laura waves the gun around and laughs.

"I warned you—warned that conniving bitch. There will be no more warnings. I've decided to teach that man-stealing whore a lesson she won't forget—one bullet and she's worm food—it's time someone did something about that conniving tramp."

Matt seems unable to move.

"Have you lost your mind? Put that gun away."

Laura looks at the gun and grins.

"I'll put it away after I plug that whore."

She looks at the gun again and then walks toward Matt as he seems to finally come out of his trance. Laura stops and glances at Matt. He notices the cold look in her face. Without thinking he grabs for the gun and she reacts. As they struggle to gain control of the gun, it goes off. Matt seems in shock as he realizes he's been shot. Laura stares at him somewhat bewildered as he falls with blood gushing from a wound in his chest.

Page **130**

"Oh my God—*Matt*—I didn't mean to. I'm so sorry. Oh God, I'm so sorry. This can't be happening—*oh God*, no."

She drops the gun and grabs her cell phone and begins dialing furiously in a panic. Matt gasps several times for air.

13

Wells Brewster hugs his sister warmly and turns around to face the driveway in front of their home. He seems upset.

"I'm gonna bust Campo really badly."

Ashley Brewster grabs Wells by the arm.

"Leave it be—I'm done with him."

Wells flexes his muscular arms and seems ready for a boxing match. He pulls his sister to him again and sighs.

"That piece of scum needs to be taught a lesson—one he won't forget anytime soon. I'm itching to pummel him."

Ashley pulls away from her brother and shoots him a cautious look as she walks toward the entrance of their sprawling home a few feet away. Wells follows her seconds later.

"That punk has no respect for women."

Ashley turns to face Wells.

"As I recall in high school you were quite a wild child—in jail just about every weekend for throwing pool parties."

Wells grins broadly.

"Uh-huh—but I had one girlfriend. I never cheated on her no matter how many times I was tempted—and it was plenty of times—I always said no—never wanted to hurt Jessica."

Ashley reacts to the name.

"How is Jessica?"

Wells gestures with her hand.

"She still lives in Castle Beach. I talk to her occasionally whenever we cross paths—she works as a reporter for a local paper—likes being part of the flow of life. I'm glad for her."

Ashley jabs Wells playfully.

"Seems you were quite upset after she turned you down when you asked her to marry you—you were lost for weeks."

Page **131**

Wells points his finger at Ashley and grins.

"I handled it quite nicely if I do say so myself. I loved her and thought she wanted to settle down and start a family."

He runs his fingers through his hair.

"I was wrong."

He points his finger at Ashley.

"But I wasn't like Campo—Jessica never had a bad thing to say about me—in fact she told me the last time we talked I was the best boyfriend she ever had—said I treated her right."

Ashley gives Wells a hug.

"I second that. You're a good brother."

Wells grins and looks around.

"Where are the folks?"

Ashley rolls her eyes.

"They're in Portland—Uncle Matt got himself into some sort of legal trouble—being sued by one of his lovers."

Wells throws his hands up in the air.

"Uh-huh—why am I not surprised at this turn of events? I swear if he wasn't dad's younger brother he'd be disowned by the rest of the family already. This is the fourth time in the last two years he's being sued because he used his celebrity status as a once-famous cyclist to bed some young guy who thought he really cared and wasn't just after a lusty one-night stand."

Ashley jabs her brother again.

"I try not to judge our uncle by his actions."

Wells laughs loudly.

"I'm not gonna pretend."

He runs his fingers through his hair again and sighs.

"That reminds me—whatever happened with dad's second cousin from Castle Beach that died during the epidemic that was all the talk a few years back? I heard she left a bit of stock in some company or something—whatever happened with that?"

Ashley seems confused and shrugs.

"I guess it went to Matt—they were pretty close. He was really upset when Shirley died. He took it really hard."

Wells grimaces as his cell phone begins to ring loudly.

"I thought I turned my phone off earlier?"
Ashley makes a lewd gesture with her finger and laughs.
"Maybe it's Jessica?"
Wells shakes his fist at her.

14

"I'm on it—relax already."
Carter Willington looks at Marla Sherwood sitting across the small cafe by herself. He shakes his head several times.
"Stop making threats—I don't respond to bullying. I told you it would take time. The girl hates me—I've got to play it cool if I want to score. She'll smell a setup from the start if I act like I just want to get between her legs. I have experience in this arena in case you forgot. Been around the block with girls plenty—of which you know given how many times you and I did the nasty in the backseat of your car—and in your bedroom. Chill already."
He grins broadly as he notices Marla gesturing with her hand to someone she's talking to on her cell phone. He smirks as he notices she seems upset. He looks down at his erection. He watches proudly as it begins to swell. Carter stifles a laugh.
"No doubt she'll be a challenge—but once I get her you'll have your revenge—her rep will be ruined forever—stained."
He smiles broadly as he hears Melissa's laughter echoing through the phone. He gestures and nods several times.

15

"Explain again how it happened?"
Will McColl looks at Laura curiously as tears continue running down her cheeks. She turns to face him and seems confused as he glances at her and at the covered body lying on a gurney. He motions to a man dressed in white and faces Laura again. He watches her reaction as Matt's body is wheeled out of the house and down the front steps to the narrow sidewalk.
"It all happened so fast—like it was all a blur."

Page **133**

Will nods and seems irritated as he sighs loudly.

"What was your husband doing with a gun?"

Laura wipes a tear from her eye.

"He bought it last year—said the area was getting sketchy and wanted to be prepared if he had to. I warned him."

Will glances at Laura curiously.

"Warned him?"

Laura nods.

"I told him it was bad idea but he wouldn't listen and then today he said he had found a use for it—said it was gonna serve its purpose—seemed pissed off about something or other."

Will watches as Laura wipes away another tear and reacts as she notices the bloodstains on the carpet. She seems about to start crying again as he reaches out to lightly pat her shoulder.

"He was going to use the gun on someone?"

Laura nods and shrugs.

"I think that's what he said—it's all a blur right now. I tried to stop him. I tried to take the gun from him and it went off."

He slowly runs his fingers through his hair.

"What happened after that?"

Laura gives him a strange look.

"I called for help—thought they'd get here in time."

She wipes away another tear and sighs.

"He stopped breathing before they showed up and then he just seemed to turn blue and then gray. Then they came."

Laura glances at the bloodstains again.

"We were thinking of having a baby."

She notices the covered body being placed inside the coroner's van. As the doors close she begins crying again.

16

Adrian looks at Elizabeth lying naked on the floor as he stands up. He grins broadly and gestures with his hand.

"This is the way it should be between us. You're my property to do as I please—it's been such a long time."

Page **134**

Elizabeth holds back tears as she watches Adrian circle her and laugh as he sees how scared she seems. He smirks.

"I'm gonna work you over no doubt—have to make up for lost time—especially after what you did to me—sending me to prison even though I was an innocent man. Oh yeah—you'll learn exactly what happens to stupid bitches that defy their boyfriends and tattle to the cops. You and I have plenty of adventures left to experience in the sack—but first I'm going to kill that dumbass boyfriend of yours. Take him out and make an example."

He grins broadly as he notices her looking at his erect penis jutting out in front of him. He makes a lewd gesture with his finger and comes toward her again. She seems frightened as he grabs her arm and pulls her to her feet. He laughs loudly.

"Uh-huh—I'm in the mood again."

He hits her hard across the face and pushes her up against the wall. She struggles but he overpowers her and begins raping her yet again—as her screams echo he laughs and plows into her without mercy. He slaps her several more times and smirks.

17
Boston

Justine Ross slowly walks back and forth on a balcony overlooking a park on Beacon Hill. She nods several times.

"It happened quickly if I recall—all sorts of weird things and then it was over—*poof*—like it never happened at all."

She looks out at the park again.

"Uh-huh—the only thing I remember Parker saying was that he never again wanted to think about what happened."

She looks at Jessica Sago on the screen of her cell phone and sighs loudly as she realizes Jessica is holding up a newspaper article from a few years back. She seems upset and shrugs.

"I don't know what else I can tell you Jessica—how about you talk to Wendy Emerson? She knows more about it than I do. I heard she told a few people that she saw Chris Gibson after he supposedly disappeared and said he was acting really weird."

Page **135**

Jessica wipes sweat from her brow.

"What do you mean Wendy saw Chris after he vanished?"

Justine walks back into her apartment and stops.

"Talk to Wendy Emerson."

Jessica reacts.

18

"Why would she say something like that?"

Diane shakes her head as she looks at Eden Penney with a mixture of pity and concern. She gestures with her hand.

"Mariska Benson is still nursing a grudge that your brother threw her over for Ashley Brewster. That girl has serious issues where Kelvin is concerned. He'd better watch his back."

Eden glances at the empty lobby area inside Springview Mall for a few seconds and faces Diane once more. She sighs.

"Mariska is going to pay for this. Like seriously, what kind of person would spread such vicious lies about me and Kelvin just because he dumped her so he could date Ashley Brewster."

Diane grins slyly and begins laughing.

"Luckily Mariska doesn't know that you and I are closer than she and I are. I never liked her anyway—especially after she tried to trick my cousin into thinking he was the father of her baby when it was actually Robert Campo who was the daddy."

Eden looks at Diane oddly.

"Mariska and Robert had a baby?"

Diane nods several times.

"Uh-huh—she aborted their baby when he refused to acknowledge he was the baby's father. Said she was a tramp and anyone could be the daddy—she had no choice after that but to pay a visit to a clinic in Portland. It devastated her that Robert didn't give a damn about her after he told her he loved her."

Diane reaches out to touch Eden's hand.

"I have something that will turn a few heads plenty."

Diane grins broadly and quickly begins pulling up photos of Robert and Mariska together. She turns and faces Eden.

Page **136**

"Are you thinking what I'm thinking Eden?"

Eden nods and grabs her cell phone and begins dialing.

"Revenge is a dish best served cold."

She watches as Diane winks at her while she clicks on each of the images with Robert and Mariska in various sexual positions in the backseat of his car—and watches with glee as they are sent to several hundred social media accounts. Diane gestures with her hand as she shuts off her cell phone with a smug look.

"Won't Mariska know you sent the photos?"

Diane begins laughing again.

"I sent them from an account I set up using a fake name from a novel called *Precipice* by **Tom Savage** that I read a few months ago. Clueless Mariska will never figure it out—not that I'm worried—she's not exactly the sharpest tool in the shed."

Eden leans toward Diane and whispers.

"How did you get a copy of those photos of Robert and Mariska doing the nasty in his car? Did he have someone take them? Like who does stuff like that? It's creepy—weird."

Diane waves her hand in the air.

"This is Robert Campo we're talking about. He's a pervert and proud of it. I bet he has plenty of others—he's friends with a freaky guy who manages a porno movie theater in Portland."

Eden seems disgusted.

"Say no more—*ugh*—gross—puke worthy."

Diane begins whispering as she looks around the empty lobby area of the mall. Her eyes briefly dance back and forth.

"He sent them to Amanda Zyperton last month—wanted her to know how good he was in bed. I thought at first it was doctored until he bragged it was him when Amanda asked about it—made it clear to her he had a really huge penis—and could easily take care of her needs—said she'd beg him to fuck her."

"*Ugh*—I never liked Robert but now I really don't. He's as disgusting as everyone says. He's as bad as Chandler."

Diane seems confused.

"Who's Chandler?"

Eden seems upset and sighs.

"He was my older brother. He's dead. I try not to think about him. He raped this girl named Ivy Patterson and then killed her. Right after that something happened to him—he died."

Diane seems in shock.

"I never knew you had an older brother. I thought it was just you and Kelvin. Thought your dad died and left you guys without any money after your estate got sued by some lawyer in Boston that specializes in rubbing rich guys into the dirt."

Eden leans back in her chair.

"Everything that happened to Kelvin and I was because of what Chandler did. He was much older than Kelvin and I—got into all sorts of trouble in Castle Beach. He ran some old guy off the road and then raped and killed his girlfriend. The old man's family and Ivy's family teamed up and hired that lawyer you mentioned from Boston. He caused my father to have a heart attack and then Kelvin and I had nothing after the estate was settled."

Diane wipes sweat from her brow.

"I knew you and Kelvin were not from Marble Hills—but I didn't know your deal—I'm sorry about your older brother."

Eden shakes her head.

"Don't be—I'm glad he's dead. He was a creep. Just like Robert Campo. Used everyone he ever knew—selfish prick."

Diane's cell phone suddenly starts to buzz.

19
Boston

Andrew Latimer looks up from his desk as loud shouting can be heard in the lobby. He stands and walks to the door. As he's about to reach for the doorknob, the door bursts open and a man comes toward him brandishing a gun. Andrew backs away as the man points a handgun at him. Jeffrey Peller sighs.

"Where is that sneaky bastard?"

Andrew seems confused.

"Who are you talking about?"

Jeffrey takes a swing at Andrew and laughs.

Page 138

"I want to see Winterfield right now."

Andrew rubs his jaw and watches as Jeffrey comes toward him again. He jams the handgun against Andrew's head.

"Get him out here—or it'll be your funeral."

He is about to hit Andrew again as Jeremy Winterfield slowly opens the door leading to his office and sees Jeffrey.

"Let him go or I'll pump your ass full of lead."

Jeffrey shoves Andrew aside and turns to look at Jeremy with hate-filled eyes. He begins laughing as he looks at his gun for a few seconds. He takes a step toward Jeremy and smirks.

"You thought you'd won—well, not quite. I'm taking you with me—if I can't be happy—neither will you. Time's up."

Jeremy looks at Andrew and then at Jeffrey.

"You'd better leave before you regret this little visit you thought no one would find out about. The police are on their way as we speak. Seems you forgot that this whole building is rigged with surveillance cameras. In addition to you losing your shirt because of not taking responsibility for your child—you're looking at a long prison stay for attempted murder. And yeah, I'm gonna press charges. Make it worse and you'll really be sorry."

Jeffrey begins laughing hysterically.

"I don't give a damn about how many cameras are covering this fucking building. I'm taking you out—you ruined my life—destroyed my marriage—and took everything from me."

Jeremy continues pointing his gun at Jeffrey as Andrew seems frozen in time as he watches the events unfolding in front of him as neither Jeffrey nor Jeremy seem ready to blink.

"I didn't mess up your life or your marriage. You cheated on your wife and made a baby with a prostitute—and then tried to deny parentage even though the DNA clearly stated you fathered the child you tried to pass off as someone else's."

Jeffrey edges closer to Jeremy.

"You're a fucking parasite. Using someone else's misery to pad your pockets—what am I supposed to do now? You took everything from me and gave it away to that skanky whore."

Jeremy rolls his eyes and seems annoyed.

"Seems you should've thought about that before you decided to go looking for entertainment outside the confines of your marriage—there are always risks to think about when you do something that hurts others—that baby deserves a shot at a good life—you on the other hand are a blight on society and decent folks everywhere who try to do the right thing while people like you go about your life using people and thinking nothing of it."

Jeffrey looks at the gun in his hand.

"That heartless whore isn't going to give a damn about that child. She's a frigging drug addict—cares only about herself and always have—that child is gonna be dead in a week."

Jeremy shoots Andrew a look and smirks.

"Do I look stupid to you? Tara Coyne didn't get one cent of the settlement. Her child was taken into custody right after the settlement was agreed upon and given to a wonderful family in Seattle. Tara has no contact with her child—I made that part of the deal in order for her not to go to jail for blackmailing you."

Jeffrey seems in shock and gestures.

"I never agreed to give up my child for adoption?"

Jeremy shakes his head.

"You refused to acknowledge paternity and in doing so you gave up all claims to the child—the case has been sealed."

"What the fuck."

He begins to tremble in rage.

"You had no right."

Jeremy glances at Andrew again.

"Uh-huh—I think I did."

Jeffrey looks at the gun again just as the police suddenly appear at the door leading to Jeremy's office with guns drawn.

"I'm not going out like this."

Jeffrey raises his gun and points it at two police officers standing less than twenty feet away. About a second later a bullet pierces his leg and he falls forward in agony. Handcuffs are slapped on him moments later as he's forced to his feet. He cries out in pain as they drag him toward the door. One of the police officers turns to face Andrew and Jeremy. He sighs loudly.

Marla stands and is about to walk toward the escalator when she sees Carter walking toward her. He grins broadly.

"Hello Marla."

She rolls her eyes.

"Get lost creep—I'm not in the mood."

Carter gestures with his hand.

"Give a guy a chance—how about we talk a bit?"

Marla watches as he edges closer to her.

"I'm a really nice guy once you get to know me. I can be quite charming—full of mystery—keep you guessing."

Marla sticks her finger in her mouth.

"*Ugh*—I'll just bet. I know exactly what you want and I'm not interested. I'm not about to fall for the load of crap you unload on the other girls in this town. Your rep isn't exactly something to be proud of—people talk—you're a lowlife."

Carter grabs Marla's arm.

"Who do you think you are—you're nothing in this town despite what you think—nothing but a lowly virgin with no game—it's time you put out for us guys—play our game."

Marla jerks free of Carter's grip. Her eyes fall to his erection straining against his faded Levi's. He grins slyly.

"I think we should visit the backseat of my car. Give me an opportunity to relieve tension—become one of my conquests."

He grabs her arm again. He pulls her toward him unaware people are watching. Marla tries to push him away. He reacts.

"I'm not taking no for an answer."

Marla angrily slaps Carter. He immediately lets go of her arm and seem in shock at the slight. He points his finger at her.

21

Alec walks back and forth across the hotel room as he seems to become more and more agitated as he paces.

Page 141

"Where the fuck is that woman—damn her."

He notices his cell phone lying on top of the counter in a small kitchenette and is about to grab it when he hears a knock on the front door. He walks toward the door in a rage. He opens the door and sees Lynne standing there. She seems upset.

"I expected you an hour ago."

Lynn continues standing in the doorway.

"I got held up in traffic. I tried calling you but your phone was off. I called you several times. I couldn't get through."

Alec runs his fingers through his hair.

"You and I have plenty to do. Like I told you earlier when we talked—I want that crazy half-sister of mine in a mental institution before the end of the week so I can claim her share of the inheritance from our father. I want it all—every cent."

Lynn seems upset as she watches him close the door and turn around to face her. He clenches his fist and sighs loudly.

"I assume you have everything ready."

Lynn nods and shows him the manuscript in her hand. She flips through it briefly as she watches his reaction. He shrugs.

"I hope that book is as good as you say it is—I want that damn bitch to be a basket case after she realizes her sordid past is going to be splashed across every sleazy tabloid in the United States and Europe. I want her suicidal. Not that it should be that far a road to cross—her whole fucking family has plenty of screws loose—starting with that bastard I call my father—from what I heard he was stark raving mad—killed people—killed one of his own daughters—and faked the death of one of his sons."

He snaps his fingers several times.

"What about your relatives? Were you able to convince them to reopen the case into their son's tragic murder?"

Lynne shakes her head and seems upset.

"They haven't responded."

Alec paces back and forth as Lynne watches him nervously. He stops and faces her again. He grits his teeth.

"Take the book with you tomorrow when you pay my dear sister a visit—make sure she sees the light. Frighten her."

Lynne glances at the manuscript and nods.

"I made a lot of accusations about what really happened to William—made it look plausible—she'll be running scared once she realizes that people will assume she killed William."

Alec dances around the room joyfully.

"Perfect—it'll just take a little nudge and she'll snap. Go off the deep end and begin babbling all sorts of junk about what really happened that day at Stanley Pier. It'll be easy to convince people she's a nutjob—make it look she helped that murderous half-sister of hers kill all those people a few years back."

Lynn nods and faces Alec.

"When do I get paid?"

Alec seems about to explode.

22

Diane shuts off her cell phone and faces Eden. She grins broadly as she folds her hands in front of her. She winks.

"That was Mariska—seems she still thinks she has the upper hand about the trash she wants to spread about you and your brother. But she'll have a nasty surprise come morning."

Eden seems confused. Diane notices.

"Come tomorrow morning everyone will be talking about the fact Mariska aborted the baby she and Robert made together and to make sure the story sticks I just released the photos of them having sex in the backseat of Robert's car using that fake email address I mentioned earlier. No one will care about what she says about you and Kelvin—this story will have more bite to it. I also plan to expose another explosive secret I know about Mariska and someone else she spread her legs for last week."

Eden seems shocked and watches Diane's demeanor change. Diane grins and makes a lewd gesture with her finger.

"Who is it? Is it Coach Holder?"

Eden looks around and whispers.

"I've heard he's done the deed with a couple of the girls from school—at least that's what Kelvin says he heard."

Page **143**

Diane gestures with her hand and laughs.

"Coach Holder has been scouting prospects for quite some time now—he's even slept with the school nurse—fucked her like a cheap hooker—took her on the examination table. Heard she got pregnant but lost the baby—husband never found out."

Diane makes a lewd gesture with her finger again.

"But that's nothing compared to what I have on Mariska."

She begins laughing and licks her lips.

"Mariska and Father Vincent have been doing the nasty in the church confessional—seems he likes things kinky."

Eden reacts in shock as Diane smiles.

23
Boston

Andrew watches as Jeremy closes the door to the office and faces him. He runs his fingers through his hair and grins.

"This was like a movie without the blood."

Andrew looks at the scattered files on the floor.

"What's going to happen to Jeffrey now?"

Jeremy shakes his head.

"He's going to be booked for assault and attempted murder. He should have simply left sleeping dogs lie."

He glances at the front door and shrugs.

"Terrible about my secretary though. She's traumatized about the whole thing. Luckily that frigging bastard didn't lay a hand on her—she'll be OK with therapy—she's tough."

Andrew wrings his hands.

"How did you remain so calm when he started to lose his mind—you didn't blink an eye—kept acting so normal."

Jeremy wags his finger at Andrew.

"I don't know—it all happened so fast."

He begins laughing.

"It never crossed my mind to fold—Peller was freaking out over what he thought I'd done—when in reality he caused what happened to him and his family by cheating on his wife."

Page 144

Jeremy runs his fingers through his hair.

"It never ceases to amaze me how people like Peller do horrible things to other people and then blame the fallout on the same people they did horrible things to. Never once did I hear Peller say he was sorry that he cheated on his wife or disgraced his children by having an extramarital relationship with a hooker when he should have been home performing the duties of a father and respectable husband. Instead he feels that everything that happened to him was my fault and the fault of his wife."

He shakes his head several times.

24

Marvin Houston opens the door to his apartment and notices eerie silence throughout the apartment. He calls out to Elizabeth several times. Seconds later he hears a sound and sees Elizabeth standing in the doorway naked. He rushes over to her and she begins crying loudly. Amid tears she tells him what happened. He reacts in shock and grabs his cell phone.

"That son of a bitch is gonna pay for what he did."

He clenches his fist as he dials. Elizabeth seems in shock as Marvin begins yelling loudly on the phone as it is picked up.

TO BE CONTINUED

A Brief Look at the Sixth Episode

Things are not what they seem as several people deal with tragic events that play out in multiple locations as a scorned wife plans the demise of her enemy while someone's world comes apart.

Episode 6
Shattered Dreams

1

Marvin Houston is talking on his cell phone when Adrian Dudley grabs him from behind. Elizabeth Pendleton screams as she watches them fall to the floor. Adrian hits Marvin several times as they both grab for a gun lying nearby. Elizabeth watches the scene unfold and finally comes to life as she manages to get the gun. Adrian whacks Marvin across the temple as he sees Elizabeth standing a few feet away with the gun in her hand. He laughs and tries to stand as Marvin lands a crushing blow to his jaw. Adrian howls in pain and they go at it for several seconds as Elizabeth nervously takes a step forward. She looks at the gun in her hand and takes another step. Adrian and Marvin continue to hit each other while she jams the gun against Adrian's back amid tears as she seems unsure of what to do next. Without warning a gunshot is heard and Adrian turns around to look at Elizabeth.

"What have you done?"

Blood gushes out from the gunshot wound in Adrian's back as Marvin reacts in shock as he looks at Elizabeth.

"You stupid bitch—you shot me."

Elizabeth looks at the gun in her hand and drops it. Adrian has a couple of spasms as he seems to be losing consciousness.

"I'll get you for this—I swear I will."

Seconds later his body goes limp. Marvin stands up and wobbles a bit as he watches Elizabeth's reaction. They look at each other for a few seconds before she collapses in his arms. A few minutes later they hear Will McColl calling out to them. He appears in the hallway with guns drawn. He notices Adrian's body lying on the floor. He silently faces Elizabeth and Marvin.

2

Alice Banning reacts in shock as she looks at her cell phone several times. She leans against the frame of the door leading to the balcony of her apartment. She sighs loudly.

"Are you sure? Are you sure she shot him?"

She almost drops the cell phone as she seems about to faint from shock. Alice takes a deep breath and grimaces.

"She's lying—he could never hurt anyone—that bitch killed him in cold blood—she murdered my sweet Matt."

She clenches her fist in anger.

"She won't get away with killing him—I won't allow her to walk away from killing the love of my life. Damn her."

She nods a few times and slowly stops to look at the cell phone in her hand. Alice realizes she's about to start crying.

3

Father Vincent looks at the sexually explicit photographs staring back at him and seems in a state of denial. He runs his fingers through his hair. He looks at the screen again. In bold lettering under the photographs is the single word BUSTED.

"Who the hell is Diana Meissen?"

His eyes travel further to the end of the email and he notices the words I KNOW EVERYTHING. He seems unable to move for a few seconds. He looks at the lurid images again.

Page 148

"This is gonna cost Nola French dearly. If that bitch thinks I'll roll over and let her blackmail me—she's got another thing coming. I'll ruin her—show her my true colors if need be."

He clenches his fist and picks up his cell phone and begins dialing. He waits a few seconds before the line is picked up.

"I think we have a problem."

He runs his fingers through his hair.

"Uh-huh—same as you—someone named Diana sent me a slew of photographs of you and me in the rectory. Uh-huh—I agree—but I actually know who really sent it to me—it was that bitch Nola French—she's playing with fire—but if she doesn't watch her step she's gonna get burned—fried to a crisp."

He glances at the computer again.

"Uh-huh—my thoughts exactly—she needs to be taught a lesson. One that is gonna make her wish she hadn't tried to play with my life—seems she needs to know exactly what happens to someone who assumes a man of the cloth is pure of heart."

He gestures with his hand and laughs.

"Uh-huh—your help is certainly welcomed."

He grins slyly.

"You and me got to find some time alone soon—I've got plenty tension now without a doubt—need a release."

He licks his lips several times.

One Day Later

4

Laura McFee fills out a few pieces of paperwork and looks at Gavin Gyston as he gathers up the papers and places them in a folder. He sighs loudly as he looks at her and seems confused.

"Is there anything else you can remember?"

Laura shakes her head.

"It all happened so fast. I'm still not sure it's real yet for me—perhaps after Matt's funeral it'll sink in and hit me."

Gavin nods several times and shrugs.

Page 149

"Again, I'm sorry about your loss."

Laura nods and turns to walk toward the door. She stops suddenly and faces Gavin again. She gestures with her hand.

"When will Matt's body be released for burial?"

Gavin shrugs and stands up.

"By noon tomorrow is my guess."

Laura nods several more times and leaves.

5

Nola French opens the door to her car parked on the side of a shaded street in front of a small supermarket. She hears footsteps behind her and as she turns around she sees Father Vincent looking at her with cold eyes. He takes a step forward.

"I think you know why I'm here."

Nola seems confused and shakes her head.

"I haven't the faintest clue."

Father Vincent grabs her by the arm and spins her around in a rage. He pushes her against the car and sighs loudly.

"You may think your little game is funny—but it isn't. I won't be blackmailed by the likes of you. I'll crush you if need be before I let someone like you destroy my life with your malicious gossip. If you cross me you'll regret it—that I promise you."

Nola jerks free of Father Vincent's grip and backs away from him. She seems frightened as she looks at him curiously.

"If you touch me again I'll have you brought up on charges—priest or no priest. Harassing someone is a crime in this state in case you let it slip your mind—ask my former husband is you don't believe me. I think you'd better leave now—before I call Will McColl and have him arrest you for assaulting me."

Father Vincent begins laughing.

"If you persist with sending me lurid pictures threatening blackmail I'll make sure you regret messing with my life."

Nola points her finger at his face.

"I don't know what you're talking about."

She gives him a knowing look and grins slyly.

Page **150**

"Nevertheless I've heard stories about you all over town concerning those late night visits from Marla Jefferson as well as all the others who shall remain nameless for the time being. I know all about your explicit escapades. That said if I were you I'd be really careful who you *entertain* at your residence when you think no one is watching. Obviously someone knows what you've been up to with some of your so-called *loyal* parishioners."

She notices his reaction and smirks.

"There's so much that the Catholic Church will tolerate nowadays in the face of intense media scrutiny—especially since they've had to cover up so much already with the endless sordid scandals involving priests such as yourself and young boys."

Father Vincent seems frozen with shock.

6

Eddie Kane knocks on the door to Elizabeth's room before he enters. She looks up and smiles weakly as Marvin walks over to Eddie and they shake hands. Eddie hands Marvin the bouquet of flowers he brought with him and walks over to Elizabeth.

"How are you doing?"

Elizabeth gestures with her hand.

"I'm just glad it's over."

Eddie sits by the edge of the bed and sighs.

"I did some checking on Adrian Dudley before I came over here. Seems he had a track record long before he met you. His records were sealed because he was still a juvenile at the time. He viciously raped a girl at a party his parents threw for his sixteenth birthday. They paid everyone to make it all go away—tried to get him admitted to a mental hospital but he vanished. They never saw him again until what happened with you. They sent their apologies when I spoke to them. Seems Dudley had a record in prison as well for bribing guards to slip him drugs and women when he could get away with it. As far as Will McColl is concerned the case is closed. His death is going to be ruled self-defense."

Marvin comes over to sit next to Elizabeth.

Page 151

"I should have been here for you."

Elizabeth takes Marvin's hand.

"You're not to blame for anything Adrian did. I owe you my life. If you hadn't shown up when you did he would've killed me—he was so cold—so distant—wanted revenge for the past."

She seems about to cry. Eddie stands up.

"David and Marvella are waiting in the lobby."

Elizabeth nods as Eddie walks to the door. He stops.

"Gina told me she'd stop by later."

Elizabeth nods once more.

7

"Uh-huh—that's right. It's time we met. Got plenty to talk about—starting with what happened in that house at Point Blye all those years ago. Seems things weren't what they seemed."

Alan McGyver seems eerily calm as he leans against the railing of the balcony overlooking the street below. He sighs.

"I think we both know that story isn't going to change reality—it's time what happened that night was dealt with."

He clenches his fist at the air. He seems worried as he wipes sweat from his brow. He shrugs and turns around.

"The minute that house is demolished the truth is going to show itself. Maybe you'd better get ready for that moment because it's coming faster than you think—next week actually."

He seems annoyed and sighs loudly.

"I'll meet you in one hour."

He shuts off his cell phone seconds later.

8

Castle Beach

"I don't know what else I can tell you—I only saw him once after he vanished—it was eerie—it was as if he was someone else—it's hard to explain. He seemed to have some sort of substance on his jeans—but it was too dark to see clearly."

Page **152**

Jessica Sago looks at Wendy Emerson curiously.

"Did he say anything? Did he ask for help?"

Wendy shakes her head several times.

"He was running after me when I ran into Juliet Sago. He stopped cold in his tracks when he saw her—scared almost."

Jessica looks at Wendy oddly.

"Juliet? You ran into my cousin that night?"

Wendy nods several times.

"I told her what I saw—but she didn't seem to believe me. I heard later she had died—it crushed me when I found out."

Jessica reacts and wipes sweat from her brow.

"I've always wondered what happened to Juliet that night. Her boyfriend freaked afterwards over what happened—he left Castle Beach right after. I think he lives in New Haven—he had family there if I recall—said only that he couldn't handle it."

Wendy seems nervous. Jessica notices.

"I closed the diner for months following what happened in Castle Beach. No one could explain anything that made sense over what occurred—some sort of virus from what I heard the CDC saying on the news—turned the bodies into a gooey mess from what they said—the press nicknamed it an Ebola twin."

Jessica watches as Wendy wrings her hands.

"What about Parker Ross and David Sherwood?"

Wendy shakes her head.

"David never discussed what happened to them that night at the Nix estate with anyone from what I heard. The only thing Parker said when I asked him about it was that he never wanted to live through what happened at the Nix estate again. Said he didn't believe in monsters before but believed that all things were possible afterwards—then clammed up right after—silent."

Jessica seems confused at the comment.

"He actually said monsters?"

Wendy nods several times and sighs.

"Took off with David after that for San Francisco—I heard they're living in Los Angeles now—working in the movies."

Jessica leans back in her chair and shrugs.

"When I was a kid people said the Nix estate was haunted—said there were weird things that happened at night."

Wendy gestures with her hand.

"I've heard all those stories too—never believed a word of it until everything went haywire—so many deaths—tragic."

Jessica gives Wendy a knowing look.

"Do you believe in ghosts?"

Wendy waves her hand in the air and sighs.

9

"How hard could bedding that bitch be?"

Melissa Marshall seems angry as she looks at herself in the rearview mirror before turning to face Carter Willington.

"Marla Sherwood is nobody's fool. She knows I'm up to something. Knows I want something from her. Got to play it cool until she lets her guard down—then I'll swoop down and take what I want from her—leave her used up and feeling cheap."

Melissa grins slyly and pulls Carter toward her.

"Step up your gameplay with that goody-goody. Once I get that miserable wretch in a vulnerable position I'll destroy her—spread tales about her everywhere—ruin her saintly rep."

She begins to giggle.

"I hate her. I really hate her."

She begins laughing as she jabs Carter.

10

Marla Sherwood pokes her head into the room as Elizabeth turns to face her. Marla takes a step forward.

"I waited until your friends left."

Elizabeth nods and motions Marla to come toward her.

"How did you get past security?"

Marla gives Elizabeth a knowing look.

"Are you seriously asking me a question like that?"

She gestures with her hand and smirks.

"I gave them the slip."

She sits by the edge of the bed. She seems upset.

"Are you all right? Did he hurt you really bad?"

Elizabeth leans against the pillow.

"It was horrible—but it's over now. Adrian Dudley will never hurt me again. I should've listened to you when you told me he was bad news. Said he had a vicious streak running through him—said I should find someone else who respected me."

Marla points her finger at Elizabeth.

"I said it as I saw it."

She looks around the room.

"Where's Marvin?"

Elizabeth glances at the door.

"He went to get me some real food. The slop they serve here is so below average. Taste like cat food—but worse."

Marla rolls her eyes.

"How would you know what cat food taste like?"

Elizabeth gives Marla a knowing look.

"Let's just say I know."

Marla wags her finger at Elizabeth.

"Marvin is a good guy—husband material."

Elizabeth nods in agreement.

"I know—he's perfect."

She looks at Marla curiously.

"How's everything going at school?"

Marla rolls her eyes and seems frustrated.

"OK. But some of the snotty kids there are so stuck on themselves. Thinks everyone must be exactly like them or there's something wrong if you choose a different route. I'm so over it actually—losers—cartoon zombies—no future—all of them."

Elizabeth wipes sweat from her brow.

"Sounds familiar—I wish I had the guts you have when it comes to dealing with your classmates. I wasn't so lucky."

She watches as Marla reacts.

"Played their twisted games and got burned—badly."

Marla reaches out to hold Elizabeth's hand.

"Do you still talk to Gina Bentley?"

Elizabeth nods several times.

"I keep in touch with Donna Markway too. She lives in Los Angeles now. Works in the movies—hobnobs with stars."

Marla sticks her finger in her mouth.

"Who cares about what famous people do?"

Elizabeth gives Marla a cautious look.

"Weren't you asking me how Ashton Markway was in real life? Wanted to meet him the next time he came to town?"

Marla's demeanor changes and she smiles.

"OK—OK—so I think he's cute."

She leans closer to Elizabeth and whispers.

"It's hard to believe he was a nerd. He looks so hot in those pictures I see in *People* magazine. Looks like he could get any girl he wanted—must have women falling all over him."

Elizabeth laughs as Marla seems confused.

11

"I'm assuming you dealt with the problem in a way that sent a very clear message. I don't like being blackmailed."

Yvette Vanderpoole watches Father Vincent's reaction and pushes him up against the wall. They kiss passionately.

"She knows I'm on to her. Nola French even went as far as to use an alias—but I didn't buy her sad excuses. I know it was her that sent those photographs of me and Mariska Benson."

Yvette looks at Father Vincent curiously.

"Are you sure it was Nola French? What if she's telling the truth and it wasn't her? What if it's someone else? Someone who's been watching you play—*watching us play*—ugh."

Father Vincent pulls Yvette toward him.

"It's Nola French—she's the only one who knows about my activities—caught me seven years ago in the confessional."

He smirks slyly and kisses Yvette. He slides his hand under her blouse and cups her breasts. They kiss several times.

"Caroline Bentley wasn't amused one bit."

Father Vincent makes a lewd gesture with his hand and pulls Yvette even closer as his hand slips under her skirt.

"She was a firecracker—couldn't get enough."

Yvette pulls away and sighs loudly.

"*Ugh*—I heard all sorts of freaky stories about her."

Father Vincent grabs Yvette again.

"Uh-huh—and they're probably all true. That woman knew all sorts of tricks—kept me guessing as we fucked."

Yvette seems upset as Father Vincent kisses her and points to a bed a few feet away. He winks slyly and laughs.

12

Gina Bentley is about to leave as she hears a knock on the door to her office. She reaches out to open the door.

"Gina Bentley?"

"Do I know you?"

Erin McHenry nods and gestures with her hand.

"I'm Erin McHenry."

Gina reacts. Erin notices.

"I hope I didn't catch you at a bad time?"

They look at each other for several seconds as Erin seems unsure of what to do next. Gina slowly extends her hand.

"I was on my way to see a friend."

Erin sighs.

"I won't take much of your time. I promise."

Gina points to her office.

"I'll try to help with what I can about my father—uh—John Bentley—as well as how I found out the truth about my true parentage following Howard Madison's suicide four years ago."

She watches as Erin takes a step forward.

13

"I expect you to pop that hateful bitch or else I'll be forced to reveal what happened between you and my cousin."

Page **157**

Carter seems frightened as he watches Melissa's finger slide across his thighs. He winces and gestures with his hand.

"I thought I told you I didn't know she was twelve. I was drunk—took her to Lake Messington and plowed her."

He sighs loudly as she smiles.

"It was dark—I thought she was our age."

Melissa makes a lewd gesture with her hand.

"Tell it to a judge."

She licks her lips and smirks.

"I'm through waiting for you to make Marla one of your many conquests. I want her reputation destroyed—totaled."

She laughs as she lets her finger slide across Carter's naked chest as he seems more frightened. He grimaces.

"I'll give you another week—then I call the cops and tell them that my ex fucked my underaged cousin last month."

Carter watches as Melissa's finger slides further until her fingers are enveloped by the thick pubic hair surrounding his exposed penis. She looks back at him and winks several times.

"Prison would be such a terrible place for someone like you—there are perverts everywhere—you'll be passed from one guy to another—traded every night for months—like candy."

Carter pulls away from Melissa.

"You'd do that to me?"

Melissa nods and laughs.

14

Christian Keller watches Amanda Zyperton smile as he shuts the door to her car. He leans forward and grins broadly.

"I had a good time. Didn't think I would but it was really nice. Malcolm is a dope for letting someone like you go."

Amanda wags her finger at Christian.

"Malcolm Kemp is old news. He said he wanted to see other people—I told him it was fine with me—I was bored with him always talking about his ex anyway—too many issues."

She reaches out to touch his hand and smirks.

Page 158

"I always thought you were cute—ever since that picture you took for school. I like guys who can fill out a fitted suit."

Christian grins broadly.

"I still have that suit in case you're wondering."

Amanda licks her lips and smiles.

"I'll call you later."

Christian nods and watches as she drives away. As the car turns the corner he notices Bruce Holland looking at him.

"Uh-huh—I see trouble ahead."

Christian walks over to where Bruce is standing when he notices the cell phone in Bruce's hand. He seems upset.

"What's that supposed to mean?"

Bruce looks at his cell phone.

"Her old man is gonna use you for target practice if you hurt his little girl—he's an expert shot from what I hear."

Christian gestures with his hand.

"I'm not afraid of Amanda's old man or the fact he teaches people how to shoot guns at Marvel's Arcade. I'm not intending to get on his bad side. I'm gonna play it careful with Amanda."

He watches Bruce's reaction and shrugs.

"I'm sick of wasting my time trying to impress girls that think they're better than me. *Ugh*—like fuck them all."

Bruce gives Christian a knowing look.

15

"I'm sorry about your sister. I should never have asked to hold a party at the beach. I'm sorry—I hope she's gonna be fine after she comes back from Boston tomorrow morning."

Kelvin Penney runs his fingers through his hair and watches as Melora Schubb wipes a tear from her eye. She turns away from him and looks out the window in the kitchen.

"I hope so too. She still has plenty of time left for them to find a way to operate without risking her life. I believe it."

Kelvin reaches out to hug Melora.

Page **159**

16
Castle Beach

"When can you start?"

Greg Petrie leans back in his chair.

"I need someone right away—today possibly."

Taylor Pendleton grins broadly and leans forward.

"I can start right now."

He stands and looks around the office.

"I'm totally open to the idea of commuting from Marble Hills until I find a place to stay—not in any rush to find a pad."

Greg wags his finger at Taylor.

"I know someone with a guest house. She's been looking to rent it out for some time now actually. I'll give her a call."

Taylor smiles broadly and nods in agreement.

17

"I know you killed Matt. I know what you did and you're not going to get away with it. I'm going to make you pay."

Alice points her finger at Laura.

"You killed him in cold blood—murdered him."

Laura rolls her eyes at Alice with contempt as they stand in the doorway of Laura's home. She seems irritated.

"Get off my property, *bitch* or I'll have you arrested for trespassing. Don't ever come back here or you'll regret it."

Alice gives Laura a sharp look.

"You're going to pay for what you did to Matt. He was a wonderful man—a gentleman—and you murdered him."

Laura points to the street.

"My husband is dead because of you—case closed—don't make things worse than they are—or I'll have you fired and run out of town. You're a vile wretched whore. You've destroyed so many marriages all over Marble Hills since you got here."

Laura takes a step forward and grimaces.

"You've made plenty of enemies."

Alice watches Laura's face crease into a wicked grin as she looks at the car parked alongside the sidewalk. Laura gestures with her hand and turns back to face Alice. She smiles slyly.

"It would be too bad if someone released those photos I found on Matt's phone. I wonder what people would say?"

Alice seems about to explode as she glances at the street and then at the cell phone in Laura's hand. She reacts.

"This isn't over—not even a little bit."

She turns and leaves. Laura begins to laugh.

18

"No one must ever tie what happened here all those years ago to us—it's been too long—too many faded memories."

Steve Pendleton turns to face the dilapidated house at the end of the weed-covered driveway as Alan stands several feet away. His eyes are intently focused on the abandoned house.

"Besides it wasn't us that did anything. It was Cliff. He was the one who left Luke Brewster in the wine cellar. Said he was gonna teach him a lesson—but then everything went wrong."

Alan grabs Steve's arm.

"Your brother locked the door to the wine cellar so Luke couldn't get out and escape. He just left him there to die."

Steve jerks free of Alan's grip.

"We don't know that for sure. Cliff told me he couldn't get the key to work. Said he tried but it broke in the lock and decided it was better not to say anything to anyone knowing Luke had already run out of air and was probably dead—told everyone that Luke ran away from home—never told anyone else what really happened—the three of us made a pact to remain silent."

Alan runs his fingers through his hair.

"Uh-huh—and look where that got us. Cliff is dead—died years ago—and now someone finally bought the property."

He faces the house again.

"It's just a matter of time before everything we've kept hidden since we were kids comes out—no place left to hide."

Page 161

Steve digs his hands into the front pockets of his jeans.

"Neither you or I had anything to do with what happened to Luke Brewster. Cliff left him to die—not us—we were outside waiting for Luke to find his way out when Cliff came and told us the key had jammed. He said he'd go for help—but he lied. Hid in the woods for several hours and then came back and swore us all to secrecy—made us promise never to tell what happened to Luke that rainy afternoon—and we never did and never will."

Steve looks at Alan cautiously.

"No one can ever know."

Alan turns away and sighs loudly.

19
Castle Beach

"Uh-huh—let me know when they leave the area. Seems someone knows what happened all those years ago to that little boy. Keep an eye on them both. It could be nothing or that they're worried the house is going to be torn down and whatever secrets lie buried in that crumbling wreckage will be exposed for all to see. I told you posting that bogus story about the estate being sold would bring out the usual suspects soon enough."

Jessica leans back in her chair and grins.

"Keep me updated."

She nods a few times and shuts off her cell phone.

"I gather someone finally took the bait—played into your hands over that listing about the old house in Marble Hills?"

Jessica turns to face Greg.

"Uh-huh—I bet there's more to this story than meets the eye. A ten-year-old boy simply doesn't disappear—unless he had help—the kind of help that always leads to several suspects."

Greg nods and seems pleased.

"What do you think really happened to the Brewster boy that even the FBI couldn't figure out? They searched the house and couldn't find anything that led them to think that he had been murdered in the house—they searched for weeks."

Jessica gestures with her hand.

"The FBI never had suspects. No one ever came forward with a ransom demand or knowledge of his whereabouts."

She glances at Greg nervously and shrugs.

"Until today that statement was absolutely true."

Greg suddenly sits up in his chair.

20
Portland

"Oh God—you're still gorgeous eye candy."

Marla Jefferson hugs Carlos Espana tightly and then steps back to admire his body. Her eyes travel down his unbuttoned plaid cowboy shirt to his snug-fitting Levi's jeans. She lets her fingers slide across the belt buckle and sighs loudly. He takes his cowboy hat off and grins broadly. She licks her lips several times as she watches his erection under his jeans beginning to swell.

"I've missed you. Missed how well you used your tongue to put me in my place. Made me so weak—tortured me."

Carlos gives Marla a knowing look.

"Since I moved back to Texas I took English classes and got myself naturalized. My wife wasn't much help but her sister was quite helpful—especially after we made a baby together."

Marla seems upset and sighs loudly.

"How's that dull wife of yours doing anyway?"

Carlos laughs noticing Marla's jealousy.

"We split after she found out I'd fathered a child with her sister. Took it hard—tried to kill her sister. She's at a correctional facility outside of El Paso for the time being—tough break."

He licks his lips and grins broadly.

"Her sister and I are still sexually involved."

Marla rolls her eyes.

"Let me guess—she thinks you're the dutiful boyfriend that has been true to her despite cheating on her sister."

Carlos begins laughing loudly.

"You said it—I didn't."

He pulls her close to him and smirks.

"I haven't forgotten about those nights we almost broke the record for lovemaking—couldn't stop—didn't try."

Marla kisses Carlos passionately.

"I'm glad you came all this way to help me with Alice Banning. She's been causing trouble for everyone. You're the only one who can bring her to her knees. She'll freak when she sees you—aware you know what she did all those years ago."

Carlos makes a lewd gesture with his hand.

"Does she know I'm back?"

Marla grins slyly.

"Not yet—I'm saving that little surprise for later in the week. When she sees the two of us together she'll know what I'm up to and from that moment I'll own her. One word from me and everyone will know what she did to her crippled father."

Carlos looks down at his erection.

"Are there any hotels nearby?"

Marla pretends to be shocked and smiles.

21

"No one else knows what happened. No one can tie us to Luke Brewster's disappearance—unless you start blabbing."

Alan gives Steve a knowing look and shrugs.

"I've lived too long with this guilt."

He runs his fingers through his hair and grimaces.

22
Portland

Marla is pinned under Carlos while he rams her repeatedly as her loud moans echo loudly throughout the hotel room for several seconds. He finally pulls out and sighs. Marla laughs.

"You certainly haven't lost your step."

"It's good to be back in New England. Lots of friends to see again—too bad Caroline Bentley met a grisly end though."

Marla seems annoyed and sighs.

"She died of a stroke in her car. She had it coming—played her husband for a fool—got too cocky—ended up dead."

She points her finger at Carlos and laughs.

"When I heard she'd croaked I felt nothing but joy if you must know. She was a nasty bitch—her death was welcomed."

Marla slides her finger across Carlos's lips.

"Heard she was fooling around with some of her late son's friends too at the time she bought the farm—so tacky."

Carlos leers at Marla knowingly.

"As if you're some sort of saint? I think we both know your deal with it comes to how you see us guys. Thinks we're all about a good time and nothing more—experimented plenty."

Marla points her finger at Carlos again.

"I admit I've been around the block more than enough times but at least I never broke any state laws when it came to bedding every good-looking guy that tweaked my fancy."

She jabs Carlos playfully.

"You're thinking about Denise Madison. That woman was worst that Caroline—you were just one of many to her."

Carlos begins laughing.

"Whatever happened to her anyway?"

Marla makes a lewd gesture with her finger.

"She's in jail—got busted for trying to break into a crypt at Crestview. It made quite a few tongues wag in Marble Hills."

She giggles and kisses Carlos.

"I'd love it if you stay in New England after I teach Alice Banning a lesson. I've missed you—missed your penis."

Carlos laughs loudly.

"How will I make a living?"

Marla kisses Carlos again and grins.

"I'll pay for your room and board—make sure you have everything you want—make sure you're well-fed. Won't expect you to remain faithful to me—won't dare tell you what to do."

Carlos makes a lewd gesture with his hand.

"This is quite a tempting offer—quite tempting."

Marla reaches out to stroke Carlos's penis.

"I'll do anything you deem necessary in order to keep you around—you have a hold on me—even after all these years."

"What about your son? He didn't exactly think much of me from what I remember. Said I was trash—threatened me."

"Chad is attending Vanderbilt at the moment. Got his hands filled with attractive classmates vying for his attention."

She reaches out to stroke his penis again and grins.

"Chad's grown a lot since his sister was murdered. Had to face reality—but he's come through untouched—knows his father and I aren't getting back together—understands my plight."

Carlos gives Marla a curious look.

23

"I just think you should read this before I start submitting it to publishers—quite the story if I do say so myself. Plenty of tragic things happen in one's life—especially murder."

Lynn Crenshaw watches Gina's reaction as she hands her the manuscript. Gina sighs loudly and seems to be in shock.

"What happened to William was an accident. I didn't kill him—he fell. It was terrible—but he fell. I didn't push him. No one thinks I did. He was showing off and he fell onto the rocks. It happened so long ago—his family said they didn't blame me."

Lynn shoots Gina a harsh glance.

"So you say."

She turns to leave.

Two Days Later

24

"Got back as soon as I could—glad to hear that there's finally been some movement about what happened to Luke."

Jessica nods as she looks at Shane Brewster for a few seconds before he sits down next to her. He looks around.

"I always suspected Steve Pendleton knew more than he told—but I'm not familiar with the other guy you mentioned—is he from Marble Hills—or possibly from Paradise Point?"

Jessica glances at the folder in front of her.

"Alan McGyver is originally from Bar Harbor—he lived in Marble Hills when he was little—moved to Chicago after his stint in the military—came back after I ran a story on Point Blye."

Shane leans closer to Jessica.

"What do we do now?"

Jessica glances at the folder again.

"I think it's time I pay Alan McGyver a visit."

Shane seems concerned.

"Shouldn't we involve the police beforehand? What if he had something to do with Luke's disappearance? Why not talk with Steve Pendleton first? We know each other—I could push him toward the edge—make him think I know what happened."

Jessica shrugs and leans back in her chair.

"I think Alan is a better bet—he seems to be the nervous type—scared about what may fall out of the woodwork."

She touches the cover of the folder.

"What if it's someone else entirely? What then?"

Shane shrugs and wrings his hands.

"Luke didn't have many friends. He was younger than Steve Pendleton—looked up to him. Followed him everywhere he went—got into all sorts of trouble from what I remember."

Jessica's cell phone begins buzzing. She looks at Shane and shoots him a cautious look as a message appears.

"It's my boss—he wants an update."

Shane nods as Jessica picks up her cell phone.

25

"I think I'm going to pay Lynne Crenshaw a visit tomorrow and see what her game is—and let know where we stand."

Gina seems upset and sighs loudly.

"What happened to William was an accident."

"I know it was Gina—but it seems Lynne Crenshaw read too many *Nancy Drew* books when she was a kid—or she's been listening to someone spin tales that are better left in the past."

Pierce Colby slowly reaches for the doorknob.

"I'll call you later."

Gina nods and wipes a tear from her eye.

26

Laura dabs her eye with a napkin as she watches the casket containing her husband's body being lowered into the ground. There are only a few people standing around the gravesite. Laura turns around and notices Father Vincent eyeing Susan Ingalls who's standing several yards away. As her eyes scan the area she sees Alice and grimaces. She sighs loudly seeing the smile that seems wreathed on Alice's face amid red lipstick.

"How dare she show up here?"

She glares at Alice and notices that she's holding something in her hand. Laura turns back to look at the open grave and seems oddly calm as she sprinkles dirt on top of the casket before the cover of the grave liner is fitted into place.

"I'm going to make you pay for what you did to Matt. If I were you I'd start planning to wear an orange jumpsuit."

Laura spins around in shock and slaps Alice in a rage.

"What about you? What about all your sordid secrets?"

Alice reacts and seems stung by the harsh words. They stare at each other coldly as everyone turns to face them.

"I have no idea what you're talking about."

Laura glances at Father Vincent.

"Really—should we ask Father Vincent?"

Alice watches as Laura walks away. She seems upset and faces Father Vincent. She gestures with her hand and shrugs.

"It wasn't Nola French that sent you those photographs. It was Laura McFee. She knows—made it quite clear just now."

Father Vincent turns to look at Laura as she gets into her car. He faces Alice again seemingly confused. She smiles.

Page **168**

27

"I think these will send chills up their spines."

Diane Gold smiles broadly as she clicks the email link and snaps her fingers several times. She closes the laptop.

"I got here as soon as I could."

Diane seems startled and sees Malcolm Kemp looking at her with a curious stare. She motions for him to sit down.

"How about you and I go somewhere?"

Malcolm grins broadly.

"I got no problem with that."

He stands.

"We could go to Portland for the day?"

Diane nods in agreement.

"I just want to be far away from Marble Hills. Robert has been following me—didn't even try to hide when I spotted him earlier outside of Springview Mall. Maybe I should talk to Chief McColl about it—have him keep an eye on Robert—scare him a bit—let him know I won't be frightened by his sick tactics."

"Is there anything I can do?"

Diane shakes her head and stands up.

28

Father Vincent looks at his cell phone for a few seconds as he stands in front of his car. He wipes sweat from his brow.

"I think you're right about Laura McFee. I just got these a second ago—these were taken late yesterday afternoon when we were leaving Sky's Diner—she's definitely our culprit."

Alice grits her teeth as she looks at the photographs of her touching the zipper on Father Vincent's pants. He grimaces.

"This isn't going to go away unless we take a stand—and put a stop to her meddling—she's out for blood—*your* blood."

She nods in agreement and grits her teeth again.

29

"Are you sure that's all she wanted?"

Eddie looks at Gina cautiously as he watches her walk to the window at the far end of her office. She turns around.

"She was really pleasant—told me about her life growing up with her adoptive parents—said they were really nice."

Gina gestures with her hand.

"She said she wanted for us to be friends—to keep in touch—seemed totally open to the idea of us hanging out."

Eddie leans back in his chair and sighs.

"I can have her followed?"

Gina wags her finger at Eddie.

"Don't you dare—the last thing I want is her thinking I'm not willing to try. If she's not who she appears to be I'll figure it out—got nothing to lose until she plays her hand of cards."

Eddie stands up and walks over to Gina.

"You already have a sister—half-sister anyway."

Gina rolls her eyes.

"I'm aware of that fact. Lindsay and I have quite a lot in common actually—but she lives in Philadelphia—remarried."

Eddie reaches out to touch Gina's shoulder.

"Philadelphia isn't that far away."

He grins broadly.

"She and Grant Monroe just had a baby. Never seen such a happy father-to-be. He's made himself at home in Philly."

Eddie looks out the window.

"Regardless, if Erin McHenry suddenly changes her tune and becomes problematic I want to know—like right away."

Gina slowly reaches out to hug Eddie and seems pleased.

"Love having a big brother in my life even if he's much too overprotective. Pierce has the same mindset as you in case you didn't know—always free with the advice—good and bad."

Eddie hugs Gina again and smiles broadly.

"I knew there was a reason I liked him."

He walks toward the door and stops suddenly.

"By the way Lynne Crenshaw should be getting a visit from one of my lawyers later today. She won't like it one bit I can assure you—he'll lay out exactly what's going to happen if she furthers her attempt to publish that worthless manuscript."

Gina nods and glances at the manuscript lying on her desk a few feet away. She seems nervous and gestures briefly.

30

Alec Martel slams his fist on top of the kitchenette counter as he watches Lynne's reaction. He seems enraged.

"That bitch sister of mine has no chance. I'll destroy her and that brother of mine too—they're gonna be sorry."

Lynne glances at Alec nervously as he comes toward her. He points his finger at her and begins laughing loudly.

"It seems I might have to take Eddie Kane out of the picture before I deal with Gina Bentley. One bullet to the back of his head will easily put an end to his overprotective behavior."

He begins laughing hysterically as Lynne seems shocked at his behavior. She glances at her manuscript on top of the coffee table nearby. Lynne reaches for it as he notices. He flies into a rage and grabs her by the arm. She begins screaming.

TO BE CONTINUED

A Brief Look at the Final Episode

Long-ago secrets from the past emerge to wreck havoc on several lives as a deranged individual recklessly plays with fire while a teenage lothario ends up on the wrong side of a gun.

Episode 7
Images from the Past

1

Carlos Espana winks at Marla Jefferson as she gives Alice Banning a knowing look as the two women stare at each other for several seconds. Marla laughs gleefully as she points at Alice.

"That's right Alice—I know what you did to your dear crippled father after he refused to give in to your blackmail scheme. You're a cold-hearted slut. Imagine pushing your father down a flight of stairs—watching him gasp for air before he finally choked to death—and for what—just to get your hands on his money—but things didn't work out for you did they? Your mother was on to your vile plan and cut you off without a red cent."

Marla grins smugly and glances at Carlos.

"Carlos was only too happy to tell me what you did to your dear father. Witnesses can be so problematic sometimes. Exactly what should I do with this juicy tidbit Alice? What should I do?"

Alice glares at Carlos.

"I should've had you deported."

Carlos laughs.

"Is that all you can say?"

He makes a lewd gesture with his finger as Marla takes a step toward Alice. She grins broadly and then licks her lips.

"I want you gone from Marble Hills by nightfall. Go back to Castle Beach—go to New York—anywhere but here."

Alice looks at Marla and Carlos.

"I don't take orders from you—either of you."

Marla pulls out her cell phone.

"One call to Will McColl and you'll be in the slammer before you can blink. Murder doesn't have a time limit. Just ask that creep that killed **Jacob Wetterling** in 1989. Bastard thought he'd gotten away with murder—and for almost three decades he lived life without worry—but sooner or later the past catches up with you—and it did for him. There's no rest for the wicked."

Alice rolls her eyes and yawns.

"I don't have to listen to this mindless dribble."

Marla looks at the cell phone.

"How about we test your theory?"

Alice sighs loudly as Marla begins dialing.

2

Katrina Kane and Lyle Lincoln walk along the surf at Bradford Beach. She slips her hand into his and grins slyly.

"I heard some of your exes are upset with you."

Lyle rolls his eyes knowingly.

"I don't care one way or the other."

He laughs.

"You're all that matters to me at this moment."

Katrina stops and faces Lyle.

"I think it's time you came for dinner at my house—get to know my folks—let them see what kind of guy you are."

Lyle seems upset and sighs loudly.

"I don't think that's a good idea—your pop might decide to wring my neck when he finds out what we did together."

Katrina laughs and playfully jabs Lyle. She notices his erection straining under his Levi's and gently strokes him.

Page 174

"I already told you my dad is all talk and no bite. He'll like you—there's nothing for you to worry about—relax already."

Lyle runs his fingers through his hair.

"I'm not gonna lie. I enjoyed what happened between us. I wanted to make love to you from the moment we first met."

He laughs as she jabs him once more.

"But you pop's a whole other matter—I know he'll rub me out the moment he finds out I took his little girl's virginity."

Katrina aggressively grabs Lyle.

"I told you already you have nothing to worry about. I make my own choices when it comes to my body. My father has no say in what I do. I wanted to be with you—wanted to give myself to you. When you first told me you intended to take my virginity I knew you were strong enough to handle me—make me see things your way. I don't regret one single moment of what happened between us. I didn't do anything I didn't want to do."

Lyle kisses Katrina lightly.

"I'm sorry the condom broke when I was inside you. If you find out you're pregnant I'll stand by you. I swear I will."

Katrina hugs Lyle warmly.

"It wasn't your fault the condom broke. It was obviously too small for your penis. I'm on the pill—always am—since I was fourteen. Don't concern yourself about it. It was no big deal."

Lyle pulls Katrina toward him.

"I'll buy bigger condoms next time."

Katrina laughs and looks at his erection again.

3

Jessica Sago watches as Alan McGyver comes toward her and sits down on the park bench. He seems a bit nervous.

"It happened so long ago."

Jessica stands up.

"Tell that to Luke Brewster's parents."

Alan grimaces. He looks around several times as if wishing he was anywhere else. Jessica notices but says nothing.

"I told you when we talked yesterday on the phone I wasn't the one that locked Luke Brewster in the wine cellar. It was Cliff Pendleton that left him there to die. Steve and I had nothing to do with what happened—it was all Cliff's doing."

Jessica points her finger at Alan.

"But you went along with it regardless—you and Steve are accessories to the death of a child—facts are facts—deal."

Alan gestures with his hands.

"What's going to happen now?"

Jessica looks at the cell phone in her hand.

"What do you think?"

They look at each other.

4

Jayne Gyston and Timothy Bradley step out of the elevator just as Diane Gold is about to get on. She gives Timothy a knowing look. He ignores her and faces Jayne as the door closes. He gestures with his hand and seems disgusted.

"Be wary of her—she's the town gossip."

Jayne wags her finger at Timothy.

"I know who she is—I know about how poisonous she can be if you cross her—Marla Sherwood warned me already."

Timothy laughs and pulls Jayne to him.

"I always liked Marla—she's nobody's fool."

They nod in agreement and walk toward the street. Jayne stops and gives Timothy an odd look. He seems confused.

"I know about the deal Bruce and Kelvin made about me."

Timothy reacts and turns away. He faces Jayne a few seconds later. He stumbles over his words for a few seconds.

"It was a stupid thing to do. I'm sorry."

Jayne looks at him for a few seconds and nods.

"It certainly was—childish. It better not happen again."

Timothy nods and faces Jayne.

"It won't happen again."

Jayne reaches out to take Timothy's hand.

Page **176**

5

Will McColl looks at the body of Lynne Crenshaw lying face down on the bed. He turns to look at the hotel clerk.

"Like I said, when she didn't come down to pay her bill I decided to find out what was going on—and found her."

Milo Tierney runs his fingers through his hair and sighs.

"I think she was strangled."

Will turns to look at Milo curiously and shrugs.

6

Robert Campo watches as Diane walks toward a nearby cafe. He clenches his fist several times and sighs loudly.

"I should've done this a long time ago."

He begins to giggle as a few people walk by.

7

Alec Martel looks up at the huge photograph of Tiffany Johnson on the side of a building and grits his teeth.

"That's my frigging money up there—wasted on some stupid teenager who never did anything for anyone."

He looks at the huge lawn in front of him covering the campus grounds that seems to go on forever. Alec laughs.

"My dear sister and I have a date with destiny."

He looks at the gun in his hand.

"No one is gonna stop me from getting what is rightfully mine. That sister of mine will never see it coming. She'll beg for mercy before I kill her—and take my rightful share. It's just a matter of time before everything falls into place perfectly."

Alec drives through the entrance and grins broadly. As he drives off someone can be seen looking at him from a distance. A mysterious figure looks up at the huge photograph. As Jeremy Weissmann turns around he seems worried and walks away.

8

"You and me have unfinished business to attend to."

Robert seems enraged as he angrily forces Diane through the double metal doors and onto a stairwell leading to the roof of Springview Mall. She tries to push him away as he laughs.

"There's only one way down from the roof, *bitch*. Plenty of dramatic scenery if truth be known—just the way you like it."

He forces her up the stairs and through another metal door. As the hot morning sun hits them they both wince. Robert twists her arm backwards and laughs loudly. He grins.

"I've waited for this moment for a long time. You and me are gonna dance—right before I throw you off the roof—splat."

Diane tries to pull free of his grip.

"I don't do homos."

Robert begins laughing.

"I'm not gay you stupid bitch—that was just a ploy to get you off your game—me and Malcolm planned the whole thing. It was perfect—until that loser began to develop feelings for you and screwed everything up. *Ugh*—who could ever like you?"

He shoves Diane toward the edge of the roof.

"If you were foolishly planning on having an open casket ceremony—forget it—it'll be a closed casket guaranteed."

He begins laughing just as a door is heard opening several feet away. They turn to see Malcolm Kemp standing there. He takes a step toward them. Robert pushes Diane closer to the edge as she screams. Malcolm seems panicked and calls out.

"Let her go. Don't be stupid. This isn't the way."

Robert begins laughing hysterically.

"I have to do it—don't you see—she made a laughingstock out of me all over Paradise Point and Marble Hills—ruined my reputation—everyone thinks I'm a freak—a sappy loser."

Malcolm glances at Diane and sighs.

"Let her go Robert. There's no way you'll get away with this. The police are already on their way. I called. It's over."

Robert twists Diane's arm and shoves her toward the edge again. She trembles as she looks down at the street below while Malcolm takes another step forward. Robert sighs.

"Go away Malcolm—forget you were ever here. Go tell everyone you saw this miserable bitch jump—no one will care if she dies—she's ruined so many lives with her endless gossiping and malicious storytelling. She deserves to die by my hand."

Malcolm edges closer to Robert.

"You'll regret it if you kill Diane. You'll get fifty to life for murdering her. You'll spend the rest of your life in prison—locked up like one of those animals at the zoo—alone and miserable."

Robert begins laughing once more.

"I'll tell everyone she jumped."

Malcolm glances at Diane and sighs loudly.

"I'll tell everyone you killed her."

Robert glares at Malcolm.

"I guess I'm gonna have to kill you too."

He pulls out a gun from his jacket pocket and laughs gleefully as he sees the shocked look on Malcolm's face.

"Say your prayers."

He laughs as he looks at the gun again.

"I hope you made your peace with your maker."

At that moment Diane elbows Robert in his chest and watches as the gun falls on the roof several feet away. As Robert tries to grab the gun Malcolm lunges at him and they struggle for a few seconds. They continue struggling to reach the gun as they move closer and closer toward the edge. Diane suddenly grabs the gun and looks at it for a few seconds before pointing it directly at Robert as he slugs Malcolm with a hard right. He stands up and takes a step forward. Robert laughs with glee.

"You don't have the guts to shoot me, *bitch*."

Seconds tick by as Diane looks at Robert trying to decide what to do when suddenly Malcolm grabs Robert from behind. They both struggle to gain control of the other and in a blink of an eye Diane sees Robert hanging from the roof as Malcolm tries to grab his arm. The bright glare of the sun obstructs his view.

"Help me. Don't let me fall. Please help."

Malcolm seems panicked.

"Please, please don't let me fall."

Before Malcolm can get a grip on Robert's hand he cries out in shock as Robert loses his grip and falls from the roof. Diane drops the gun as she turns to look at Malcolm aware of what happened seconds ago. Slowly they both look over the edge.

9

"Alice was fit to be tied when she realized she'd lost and I'd won—she looked like she'd just lost her best friend."

Marla begins laughing as she slowly slides her fingers across Carlos's naked chest. She kisses him several times.

"I think I should add some more injury to her bruised ego just for good measure—would be quite a coup if I got her mother to press charges against her. There's no love lost between them after what she did. Poor Alice lost everything after her mother kicked her out of the house for causing her father's death."

Marla gives Carlos a smug look and laughs.

"No wonder Alice ended up working as a waitress—what other skills did she have—from riches to rags—*how sad.*"

She sits up in bed and grabs her cell phone.

"Uh-huh—yeah—I think I should give her mother a call."

Marla begins dialing. Carlos seems upset.

"You've won. She's lost. Let it go."

Marla turns to look at Carlos.

"I want her destroyed—ruined—stripped of her game forever—she caused me so much trouble with Matt McFee and Steve Pendleton—always spreading her legs—playing them for fools knowing how easy they were to be misled. I hate her."

Carlos pulls Marla toward him and grins.

"Forget those guys—you've got me in your bed and between your legs—she has nothing. She's been bested."

Marla seems upset and gestures. She faces Carlos and leans over to kiss him. She traces her finger across his lips.

Page **180**

"Matt is no threat to you anymore—he's dead—murdered a few days ago—his wife killed him—shot him by accident."

Carlos reaches out to stroke Marla's cheek. He seems relieved hearing that Matt is dead. He kisses her on the cheek.

"What about Steve Pendleton?"

"He's just a friend with benefits—nothing more."

Carlos lies back in bed and sighs loudly.

"I want you all to myself. No other men in your bed."

Marla seems annoyed.

"What about you? Will there be other women in your bed other than me? I thought you and I had an agreement?"

Carlos makes a lewd gesture with his finger.

"It's different with men. We get to play. Our women are to remain true to us—never wandering from bed to bed."

Marla seems upset at the comment.

10

Scott Millner turns the body over and faces Diane and Malcolm a few seconds later. He shakes his head and shrugs.

"Dead—the fall broke his neck. No pain."

Malcolm reaches out to comfort Diane as Scott stands up and gestures to the coroner waiting a few yards away. He wrings his hand and faces Diane and Malcolm again. He seems upset.

"Did he say much of anything before he fell?"

Diane shakes her head. Malcolm mumbles a few words and turns away. Scott looks at them curiously and sighs.

11

Father Vincent watches as Susan Ingalls pulls up her skirt and faces him. He grins broadly and point to the door nearby.

"I'll call you tomorrow."

Susan nods and watches as he leaves. She continues looking at him as he walks down the walkway to his car. From a distance she sees Melissa Marshall waving to Father Vincent.

Page **181**

"That whore is shameless. Damn her."

Susan seems enraged as she watches them embrace passionately a few seconds later. Susan grits her teeth as she watches them talk briefly before Melissa begins unzipping Father Vincent's pants. Susan clenches her fist and turns away.

"Maybe it's time I call Monsignor Holbrook and tell him that Father Vincent has strayed with Melissa—make it look like he took advantage of her—and broke his vows to the church."

She begins giggling as she watches them.

12

Eddie Kane is about to pick up his cell phone just as a cold blast of wind shoots through the room. Every window in his office snaps shut without warning. He looks around and sighs.

13

"Seems you and I have been playing games with each other. But I think we both know I'm gonna get my way."

Carter Willington winks slyly at Marla Sherwood as he begins unbuttoning his jeans. She looks at him and laughs.

"This isn't going to happen."

He grabs Marla and pushes her against the wall of the locker room. He grins broadly as he sees her shocked reaction.

"You've played your hand of cards—and you've lost. I want you and there's nothing that's going to stop me from adding you to my long list of conquests. A guy can only put up with enough excuses from a girl like you—until he finally takes charge."

Marla looks at the empty rows of lockers and seems oddly quiet as he tries to press his face to hers. He notices her cold stare and begins laughing. He points his finger at her and smirks.

"When I'm done sticking you there'll be no more excuses from you—you'll put out every day I want a piece. You'll get to know my moods soon enough—give me lots of blowjobs."

"Is that what you think will happen?"

Page 182

He nods as he attempts to kiss her. Without warning she kicks him in the groin and watches with glee as he doubles over with pain. She stands there for a few seconds looking at him with her hands on her hips. He looks up at her and grimaces.

"Fucking bitch—you're gonna pay for this."

Marla makes a lewd gesture with her hand and points at him as he tries to stand. She glances at the door nearby.

"I told you I wasn't like the other girls in this town—you should've believed me the first time I said it—seen the light."

She turns to leave. He grimaces again.

14

Will McColl looks at the paperwork in front of him and sighs loudly. He closes the folder and stands up. He sighs.

"She won't be pleased to see me."

He stands and faces the front door. Seconds later he leaves just as the phone on top of the desk begins ringing.

15

"It's just you and me dear sister. There's no one coming to save you—seems the security team got an urgent call."

Alec begins laughing slyly as he circles Gina Bentley.

"Uh-huh—they're out on a wild goose chase on the other side of this godforsaken campus. Of course that leaves you at my mercy—to do with as I please unless I get what I want—what was mine before you foolishly used it to finance this stupid school."

Gina seems unable to move as Alec takes a step forward. He grins broadly as he waves a gun at her. He begins laughing.

"I want it all—every penny."

He takes another step forward. He notices her panicked look and smirks. He points the gun at her and licks his lips.

"That bastard never wanted to know me—but guess what sister dearest—our dear father and I are one in the same."

He looks at the gun in his hand again.

16

Laura McFee appears in shock as she's led from the front steps of her house as onlookers react and begin whispering.

"Not everything is what it appears to be."

Will sighs loudly and watches as she's placed inside a police car. Laura angrily turns to look at Will. The scowl on her face says it all as the door is closed. He sighs and turns away.

"She probably thought no one would ever find out what really happened that day—so much for wishful thinking."

Will gives Nola French a strange look as he faces her.

"I had no idea. It never crossed my mind."

She turns to look at Laura briefly before noticing several people pointing to the house a few feet away. Nola continues standing on the sidewalk as Will gets into his police car.

17

"You'll never get away with this. Eddie will figure it out and have you put away. You'll spend the rest of your life in prison for killing me—he'll make sure of it. He'll never give up."

Alec begins laughing hysterically and points at Gina.

"He's next on my list. Eddie Kane won't be much help to anyone if he's got a bullet in his head courtesy of yours truly."

He slowly looks around the office and grimaces.

"You wasted my money on a frigging school for poor slobs from the worst families across the country—how dare you."

Gina seems confused and gestures.

"I didn't know about you."

Alec seems enraged as he looks at the gun in his hand and then again at the lavishly decorated room. He shrugs.

"I'll just bet you didn't."

He begins laughing hysterically again.

"Jennifer Parker should've killed you when she had the chance. She and I would've made quite a pair no doubt."

"You just might get your wish."

Alec spins around and reacts in shock as he sees Tiffany Johnson standing about ten feet away. She grins broadly seeing his shocked expression. Alec rubs his eyes several times.

"Who the hell are you?"

Tiffany laughs and takes a step forward as Gina watches in amazement. Tiffany smirks slyly and gives Alec a knowing look.

"I think you know exactly *who* I am—don't you."

Alec seems to realize at that moment what's happening before his eyes and looks at the gun in his hands. He grins.

"I'm not afraid of you."

Tiffany folds her hands across her chest.

"Are you sure about that?"

Tiffany turns around to look at Gina briefly and faces Alec again. She takes another step forward. He seems nervous.

"If you take one more step I'll be forced to."

Tiffany begins laughing as she edges closer to Alec seeing the panic in his face becoming more and more apparent.

18

Steve Pendleton stares at the walls of the tiny room just as Gavin Gyston enters the room. Steve seems visibly upset.

"Like I said earlier, I didn't kill Luke Brewster. It was my brother—he locked him in the wine cellar. I didn't do it."

Gavin shoots Steve a knowing look.

"But you kept your mouth shut all these years—and that makes you an accessory to what happened to that little boy. You could've said something but you didn't—never even tried."

Steve reacts and watches as Gavin sits down at the desk and opens a box containing several thick folders. He shrugs.

"I think you'd better tell me everything."

He coldly glances at Steve and sighs.

"I don't have all day."

Steve wipes sweat from his brow.

"It wasn't my fault—it was Cliff. He did it."

Gavin seems annoyed and slams his fist down on the table. Steve turns to look at the door. Gavin grabs his arm.

"You'd better start talking buddy—the evidence against you is staggering. It doesn't look good—not even a little bit."

Steve runs his fingers through his hair.

19

Maxwell Pendergraft grins broadly as the door opens and Charlene McColl throws her arms around him. They hug warmly for several seconds. He glances at her swollen stomach.

"I guess I'm a few days early?"

Charlene shakes her fist at her brother.

"I missed you so much."

They hug warmly again for a few minutes as Maxwell gives Charlene a knowing look and smirks. She notices and jabs him playfully. He laughs loudly as she jabs him several times.

"What are you up to big brother?"

He turns to look at the front door as it opens.

20

"I just want to say again how sorry I am about what happened with Robert. I had no idea he was so deranged."

Diane seems oblivious to Malcolm as she stares at a cup of coffee in her hand. She finally looks away and sighs loudly.

"His eyes were so full of hate."

She looks at the cup of coffee again.

"It was like one of those horror movies where someone just snaps and starts blindly killing everyone around them."

Malcolm reaches out to touch Diane's hand.

21

Eddie bursts through the door leading to Gina's office and stands frozen in shock as he looks at the scene in front of him.

"Gina? Are you OK? Is this?"

In one corner of the room Alec is crouched in a ball-like position as his eyes continues darting back and forth seeing something or someone that isn't visible to the naked eye. Eddie turns to face Gina seconds later. Her face is a mixture of shock and joy as she looks at Alec. Eddie slowly takes a step forward.

"I got here as soon as I could. Jeremy Weissmann paid me a visit earlier—told me to get over here in order to stop—said you were in danger—said someone was here—someone evil."

He glances at Alec again and sighs.

"Alec Martel I assume?"

Gina nods and runs to Eddie. They embrace for several seconds as she looks at Alec again. He continues babbling.

"Tiffany Johnson was just here. She did something to him—there was a flash—it blinded me for a few seconds—I couldn't see. Then she was gone as if she was never here."

Eddie wipes sweat from his brow.

"Did she say anything to you?"

Gina shakes her head and glances at Alec.

"He showed up saying he was going to kill me and take his rightful place here in Marble Hills—said he was going to kill you too—made quite a show of the fact—seemed really smug."

Eddie runs his fingers through his hair.

"Will is on his way—he shouldn't be too long."

He looks at Alec again and then faces Gina. He seems nervous as he looks at the gun lying on the floor nearby.

"I think it's best if we left out Tiffany's visit when we talk to Will McColl—don't need to start tongues wagging again."

Gina nods in agreement.

"What do you think she did to him?"

Eddie glances at Alec and shrugs.

"Don't know and don't really care one way or the other. I'm just really thankful she was looking out for you yet again."

Gina pulls away from Eddie and sighs loudly.

"I wish I could thank her."

She looks at Alec again and then Eddie.

"Do you think she's still here?"

Eddie wags his finger at Gina. They share a curious glance and hug once more just as Will suddenly appears at the door.

22
One Week Later

Susan seems pleased as Father Vincent grabs a cardboard box and follows her through the front door of her home.

"I'm so sorry about what happened to you."

She reaches out to stroke his belt buckle and seductively licks her lips. He grins broadly and then glances back at his car parked in the driveway. He gestures with his hands briefly.

"It'll just be for a month or so—until I can figure out what I'm going to do for a job now since I'm no longer a priest."

Susan pulls Father Vincent to her.

"I don't mind one bit—having you in my bed isn't going to be a problem whatsoever. I'm looking forward to it actually."

Father Vincent seems pleased and smirks.

"From now on you can call me Vinnie. I'm just Vincent Pogozi from today onward—Vinnie from Boston actually."

Susan grins broadly and lets her fingers slide down to the buttons on his Levi's. She looks at him cautiously and sighs.

"Do you know who told on you?"

Vincent shakes his head and grimaces.

"I don't—at least not yet. But if that bitch Nola French outed me I'll teach her a lesson—one that she won't forget."

Susan grins and begins unbuttoning his jeans.

"If you need my help just let me know."

He grins slyly as he watches her fingers cautiously probing his erection straining against the confines of his boxer briefs.

"I might just take you up on that offer."

Susan looks at Father Vincent and licks her lips.

"I'd do anything for you. I swear on my life."

"You and I are gonna be spending a lot of time in bed."

"I've loved you for such a long time Vinnie."

Page **188**

Susan pushes Father William against a wall. They kiss for a few seconds. She strokes his erection again and smiles slyly.

"What about Melissa Marshall?"

"What about her? Why do you ask?"

Susan seems bothered by the comment.

23

Eddie and Gina stand at the top of the courthouse steps as Alec is led away clad in a straitjacket—while several reporters descend en masse on the plain-looking white van with the words BROOKHAVEN HOSPITAL stenciled in bold letters on both sides. Gina seems worried as she watches the drama slowly unfold.

"Do you think he's faking being mentally ill?"

Eddie turns to look at Gina and smirks.

"If he's faking it won't do him any good. I made a deal with the prosecutor's office that he can't be let out unless I'm made aware of it months in advance. It was a really easy sell."

He grins broadly and snaps his fingers.

"I got myself appointed his guardian since he has no other living relatives left in Bermuda. Before he can be set free I would have to approve his release—and that approval is based on how mentally fit I deem him to be. Bet Alec didn't think of an outcome like that while he was setting his schemes in motion after finding out he was heir to the Madison fortune—and before he poisoned his parents and killed his girlfriend in a fit of blind rage."

Gina watches as the van drives away.

Page **189**

About the Series Creator

Gary Brin was born in 1965 and has lived in the United States Virgin Islands, Hawaii and California. He has edited numerous original literary works over the years—both new and revised. In 2019 he established Standish Press to bring forth interesting fictional and historical material usually ignored by mainstream publishers because of specific views or content. In addition to publishing books, he also created the Nancy Hanks Lincoln Public Library (named after the mother of Abraham Lincoln) in 2014 to make available hard-to-find books to a worldwide audience.

Production Notes

Written by Wesley Adams and Daphne McGee
Manuscript edited by Gary Brin
Cover photograph from Adobe Stock Images
Front cover design and interior book layout by Gary Brin
Cover layout by Victoria Valentine
Additional help provided by Carlton J. Young
Series created by Gary Brin

Character List

Lacey Arlington
Dane Ayler
Alice Banning
Mariska Benson
Marlene Benson
Riley Benson
Gina Bentley
Timothy Bradley
Ashley Brewster
Shane Brewster
Wells Brewster
Dina Brown
Robert Campo
Pierce Colby
Lynne Crenshaw
Marvella DuBois
Adrian Dudley
Wendy Emerson
Carlos Espana
Nola French
Patrick Gibbs
Diane Gold
Gavin Gyston
Jayne Gyston
Wanda Gyston
Carissa Holder
Trey Holder
Bruce Holland
Simone Holland
Marvin Houston
Susan Ingalls
Kent Jefferson

Marla Jefferson
Tiffany Johnson
Eddie Kane
Katrina Kane
Christian Keller
Malcolm Kemp
Andrew Latimer
Lyle Lincoln
Warren Manning
Gable Markway
Liza Marshall
Melissa Marshall
Alec Martel
Charlene McColl
Will McColl
Laura McFee
Matt McFee
Alan McGyver
Erin McHenry
Jon Melchoir
Scott Millner
Jeffrey Peller
Maxwell Pendergraft
Elizabeth Pendleton
Steve Pendleton
Taylor Pendleton
Eden Penney
Kelvin Penney
Greg Petrie
Vincent Pogozi
Justine Ross
Jessica Sago
David Sawyer
Melora Schubb
Natalie Selleck
Marla Sherwood
Denver Skiffington
Todd Spencer

Milo Tierney
Megan Vanderpoole
Yvette Vanderpoole
Jeremy Weissmann
Adam Westerfeldt
Carter Willington
Steve Willington
Jeremy Winterfield
Amanda Zyperton

Real People Mentioned

Carrie Fisher
Anne Frank
Otto Frank
Irene Garza
Nancy Hanks Lincoln
Colleen McCullough
Grace Metalious
Martha Mitchell
Debbie Reynolds
Tom Savage
Gilbert Stuart
Milo Ventimiglia
Jacob Wetterling

Next in the Series
Book 9
Virgin Islands

Standish Press